Oboram King of Fayeries

The Scottish History of Jmaes the Fourth

Oboram King of Fayeries

The Scottish History of Jmaes the Fourth

1st Edition | ISBN: 978-3-75239-234-0

Place of Publication: Frankfurt am Main, Germany

Year of Publication: 2020

Outlook Verlag GmbH, Germany.

Reproduction of the original.

THE SCOTTISH HISTORY OF JAMES THE FOURTH

by
Oboram King of *Fayeries*

Musicke playing within. *l. Chor.*

Enter After Oberõ, *King of Fayries, an Antique, who dance about*
a Tombe, plac'st conueniently on the Stage, out of the which, suddainly
starts vp as they daunce, Bohan *a Scot, attyred like a ridstall*
man, from whom the Antique flyes.   Oberon *Manet.*

Bohan.

Ay say, whats thou?

Oberon. Thy friend *Bohan.*

   Bohan. What wot I, or reck
I that, whay guid man, I reck
no friend, nor ay reck no foe, als 10
ene to me, git the ganging, and
trouble not may whayet, or ays
gar the recon me nene of thay friend, by the mary masse sall I.

   Ober. Why angrie Scot, I visit thee for loue: then what
mooues thee to wroath?

   Bohan. The deele awhit reck I thy loue. For I knowe
too well, that true loue tooke her flight twentie winter sence to
heauen, whither till ay can, weele I wot, ay sal nere finde loue:
an thou lou'st me, leaue me to my selfe. But what were those
Puppits that hopt and skipt about me year whayle? 20

   Oberon. My subiects.

   Boh. Thay subiects, whay art thou a King?

   Ober. I am.

   Bohan. The deele thou art, whay thou look'st not so big as
the king of Clubs, nor so sharpe as the king of Spades, nor so
faine as the king Adaymonds, be the masse ay take thee to bee
the king of false harts: therfore I rid thee away, or ayse so curry
your Kingdome, that yous be glad to runne to saue your life.

   Ober. Why stoycall Scot, do what thou dar'st to me, heare is
my brest strike. 30

   Boh. Thou wilt not threap me, this whiniard has gard many
better mẽ to lope thẽ thou: but how now? Gos sayds what wilt
not out? whay thou wich, thou deele, gads sute may whiniard.

2

Ober. Why pull man: but what an twear out, how then?

Boh. This then, thou weart best begon first: for ayl so lop
thy lyms, that thouse go with half a knaues carkasse to the deele

Ober. Draw it out, now strike foole, canst thou not?

Boh. Bread ay gad, what deele is in me, whay tell mee thou
skipiack what art thou?

Ober. Nay first tell me what thou wast from thy birth, what 40
thou hast past hitherto, why thou dwellest in a Tombe, & leauest
the world? and then I will release thee of these bonds, before
not.

Boh. And not before, then needs must needs sal: I was borne
a gentleman of the best bloud in all *Scotland*, except the king,
when time brought me to age, and death tooke my parents, I
became a Courtier, where though ay list not praise my selfe, ay
engraued the memory of *Boughon* on the skin-coate of some of
them, and reueld with the proudest.

Ober. But why liuing in such reputation, didst thou leaue to 50
be a Courtier?

Boh. Because my pride was vanitie, my expence losse, my reward
faire words and large promises, & my hopes spilt, for that
after many yeares seruice, one outran me, and what the deele
should I then do there. No no, flattering knaues that can cog
and prate fastest, speede best in the Court.

Ober. To what life didst thou then betake thee?

Boh. I then chang'd the Court for the countrey, and the wars
for a wife: but I found the craft of swaines more vile, then the
knauery of courtiers: the charge of children more heauie then 60
seruants, and wiues tongues worse then the warres it selfe: and
therefore I gaue ore that, & went to the Citie to dwell, & there
I kept a great house with smal cheer, but all was nere the neere.

Ober. And why?

Boh. because in seeking friends, I found table guests to eate
me, & my meat, my wiues gossops to bewray the secrets of my
heart, kindred to betray the effect of my life, which when I noted,
the court ill, the country worse, and the citie worst of all, in
good time my wife died: ay wood she had died twentie winter
sooner by the masse, leauing my two sonnes to the world, and 70
shutting my selfe into this Tombe, where if I dye, I am sureI

3

am safe from wilde beasts, but whilest I liue, cannot be free frõ ill companie. Besides, now I am sure gif all my friends faile me, I sall haue a graue of mine owne prouiding: this is all. Now what art thou?

Ober. Oberon King of Fayries, that loues thee because thou hatest the world, and to gratulate thee, I brought those Antiques to shew thee some sport in daunsing, which thou haste loued well.

Bohan. Ha, ha, ha, thinkest thou those puppits can please 80 me? whay I haue two sonnes, that with one scottish gigge shall breake the necke of thy Antiques.

Ober. That would I faine see.

Boha. Why thou shalt, howe boyes.

Enter Slipper and Nano.

Haud your clacks lads, trattle not for thy life, but gather vppe your legges and daunce me forthwith a gigge worth the sight.

Slip. Why I must talk on Idy fort, wherefore was my tongue made.

Boha. Prattle an thou darst ene word more, and ais dab this 90 whiniard in thy wembe.

Ober. Be quiet *Bohan*, Ile strike him dumbe, and his brother too, their talk shal not hinder our gyg, fall to it, dance I say mã.

Boh. Dance Humer, dance, ay rid thee.

The two dance a gig deuised for the nonst.

Now get you to the wide world with more thẽ my father gaue me, thats learning enough, both kindes, knauerie & honestie: and that I gaue you, spend at pleasure.

Ober. Nay for their sport I will giue them this gift, to the Dwarfe I giue a quicke witte, prettie of body, and awarrant his 100 preferment to a Princes seruice, where by his wisdome he shall gaine more loue then cõmon. And to loggerhead your sonne, I giue a wandering life, and promise he shall neuer lacke: and auow that if in all distresses he call vpon me to helpe him: now let them go.

Exeunt with curtesies.

Boh. Now King, if thou bee a King, I will shew thee whay I

4

hate the world by demonstration, in the year 1520. was in
Scotland, a king ouerruled with parasites, mifled by lust, & many
circumstances, too long to trattle on now, much like our 110
court of *Scotland* this day, that story haue I set down, gang with
me to the gallery, & Ile shew thee the same in Action, by guid
fellowes of our country men, and then when thou seest that,
iudge if any wise man would not leaue the world if he could.

    Ober. That will I see, lead and ile follow thee.   *Exeunt.*

      Laus Deo detur in Eternum. *i. i.*

Enter the King of England, the King of Scots, Dorithe *his Queen,
the Countesse, Lady* Ida, *with other Lords. And* Ateukin *with
them aloofe.*

      Attus primus. Scena prima. 120

  K. of Scots. Brother of England, since our neighboring land,
And neare alliance doth inuite our loues,
The more I think vpon our last accord,
The more I greeue your suddaine parting hence:
First lawes of friendship did confirme our peace,
Now both the seale of faith and marriage bed,
The name of father, and the style of friend,
These force in me affection full confirmd,
So that I greeue, and this my heartie griefe 130
The heauens record, the world may witnesse well
To loose your presence, who are now to me
A father, brother, and a vowed friend.

  K. of Eng. Link all these louely stiles good king in one,
And since thy griefe exceeds in my depart,
I leaue my *Dorithea* to enioy, thy whole compact
Loues, and plighted vowes.
Brother of *Scotland*, this is my ioy, my life,
Her fathers honour, and her Countries hope,
Her mothers comfort, and her husbands blisse: 140
I tell thee king, in louing of my *Doll*,
Thou bindst her fathers heart and all his friends
In bands of loue that death cannot dissolue.

  K. of Scots. Nor can her father loue her like to me,
My liues light, and the comfort of my soule:
Faire *Dorithea*, that wast Englands pride,
Welcome to *Scotland*, and in signe of loue,

Lo I inuest thee with the Scottish Crowne.
Nobles and Ladies, stoupe vnto your Queene.
And Trumpets sound, that Heralds may proclaime, 150
Faire *Dorithea* peerlesse Queene of Scots.

   All. Long liue and prosper our faire Q. of Scots.

                                       Enstall and Crowne her.

   Dor. Thanks to the king of kings for my dignity,
Thanks to my father, that prouides so carefully,
Thanks to my Lord and husband for this honor,
And thanks to all that loue their King and me.

   All. Long liue faire *Dorithea* our true Queene.

   K. of E. Long shine the sun of *Scotland* in her pride,
Her fathers comfort, and faire *Scotlands* Bride. 160
But *Dorithea*, since I must depart,
And leaue thee from thy tender mothers charge,
Let me aduise my louely daughter first,
What best befits her in a forraine land,
Liue *Doll*, for many eyes shall looke on thee,
Haue care of honor and the present state:
For she that steps to height of Maiestie,
Is euen the marke whereat the enemy aimes.
Thy vertues shall be construed to vice,
Thine affable discourse to abiect minde. 170
If coy, detracting tongues will call thee proud:
Be therefore warie in this slippery state,
Honour thy husband, loue him as thy life:
Make choyce of friends, as Eagles of their yoong,
Who sooth no vice, who flatter not for gaine:
But loue such friends as do the truth maintaine.
Thinke on these lessons when thou art alone,
And thou shalt liue in health when I am gone.

   Dor. I will engraue these preceps in my heart,
And as the wind with calmnesse woes you hence, 180
Euen so I wish the heauens in all mishaps,
May blesse my father with continuall grace.

   K. of E. Then son farwell, the fauouring windes inuites vs to depart.
Long circumstance in taking princely leaues,
Is more officious then conuenient.
Brother of *Scotland*, loue me in my childe,

6

You greet me well, if so you will her good.

K. of Sc. Then louely *Doll*, and all that fauor me,
Attend to see our English friends at sea,
Let all their charge depend vpon my purse: 190
They are our neighbors, by whose kind accord,
We dare attempt the proudest Potentate.
Onely faire Countesse, and your daughter stay,
With you I haue some other thing to say.

> *Exeunt all saue the King, the Countesse,*
> Ida, Ateukin, *in all royaltie.*

K. of S. So let them tryumph that haue cause to ioy,
But wretched King, thy nuptiall knot is death:
Thy Bride the breeder of thy Countries ill,
For thy false heart dissenting from thy hand, 200
Misled by loue, hast made another choyce,
Another choyce, euen when thou vowdst thy soule
To *Dorithea*, Englands choyseff pride,
O then thy wandring eyes bewitcht thy heart,
Euen in the Chappell did thy fancie change,
When periur'd man, though faire *Doll* had thy hand,
The Scottish *Idaes* bewtie stale thy heart:
Yet feare and loue hath tyde thy readie tongue
From blabbing forth the passions of thy minde,
Lest fearefull silence haue in suttle lookes 210
Bewrayd the treason of my new vowd loue,
Be faire and louely *Doll*, but here's the prize
That lodgeth here, and entred through mine eyes,
Yet how so ere I loue, I must be wise.
Now louely Countesse, what reward or grace,
May I imploy on you for this your zeale,
And humble honors done vs in our Court,
In entertainment of the English King.

Countesse. It was of dutie Prince that I haue done:
And what in fauour may content me most, 220
Is, that it please your grace to giue me leaue,
For to returne vnto my Countrey home.

K. of Scots. But louely *Ida* is your mind the same?

Ida. I count of Court my Lord, as wise men do,
Tis fit for those that knowes what longs thereto:

Each person to his place, the wise to Art,
The Cobler to his clout, the Swaine to Cart.

 K. of Sc. But *Ida* you are faire, and bewtie shines,
And seemeth best, where pomp her pride refines.

 Ida. If bewtie (as I know there's none in me) 230
Were sworne my loue, and I his life should be:
The farther from the Court I were remoued,
The more I thinke of heauen I were beloued.

 K. of Scots. And why?

 Ida. Because the Court is counted *Venus* net,
Where gifts and vowes for stales are often set,
None, be she chaste as *Vesta*, but shall meete
A curious toong to charme her eares with sweet.

 K. of Scots. Why *Ida* then I see you set at naught,
The force of loue. 240

 Ida. In sooth this is my thoght most gratious king,
That they that little proue
Are mickle blest, from bitter sweets of loue:
And weele I wot, I heard a shepheard sing,
That like a Bee, Loue hath a little sting:
He lurkes in flowres, he pearcheth on the trees,
He on Kings pillowes, bends his prettie knees:
The Boy is blinde, but when he will not spie,
He hath a leaden foote, and wings to flie:
Beshrow me yet, for all these strange effects, 250
If I would like the Lad, that so infects.

 K. of Scots. Rare wit, fair face, what hart could more desire?
But *Doll* is faire, and doth concerne thee neere.
Let *Doll* be faire, she is wonne, but I must woe,
And win faire *Ida*, theres some choyce in two.
But *Ida* thou art coy.

 Ida. And why dread King?

 K. of Scots. In that you will dispraise so sweet
A thing, as loue, had I my wish.

 Ida. What then? 260

 K. of Scots. Then would I place his arrow here,
His bewtie in that face.

Ida. And were *Apollo* moued and rulde by me,
His wisedome should be yours, and mine his tree.

K. of Scots. But here returnes our traine.
Welcome faire *Doll*: how fares our father, is he shipt and gone.

Enters the traine backe.

Dor. My royall father is both shipt and gone,
God and faire winds direct him to his home.

K. of Sc. Amen say I, wold thou wert with him too: 270
Then might I haue a fitter time to woo.
But Countesse you would be gone, therfore farwell
Yet *Ida* if thou wilt, stay thou behind,
To accompany my Queene.
But if thou like the pleasures of the Court,
Or if she likte me tho she left the Court,
What should I say? I know not what to say,
You may depart, and you my curteous Queene,
Leaue me a space, I haue a waightie cause to thinke vpon:

Id., it nips me neere: 280
It came from thence, I feele it burning heere.

Exeunt all sauing the King and Ateukin.

K. of Scot. Now am I free from sight of commõ eie,
Where to my selfe I may disclose the griefe
That hath too great a part in mine affects.

Ateu. And now is my time, by wiles & words to rise,
Greater then those, that thinks themselues more wise.

K. of Scots. And first fond King, thy honor doth engraue,
Vpon thy browes, the drift of thy disgrace:
Thy new vowd loue in sight of God and men, 290
Linke thee to *Dorithea*, during life.
For who more faire and vertuous then thy wife,
Deceitfull murtherer of a quiet minde,
Fond loue, vile lust, that thus misleads vs men,
To vowe our faithes, and fall to sin againe.
But Kings stoupe not to euery common thought,
Ida is faire and wise, fit for a King:
And for faire *Ida* will I hazard life,
Venture my Kingdome, Country, and my Crowne:
Such fire hath loue, to burne a kingdome downe. 300
Say *Doll* dislikes, that I estrange my loue,

9

Am I obedient to a womans looke?
Nay say her father frowne when he shall heare
That I do hold faire *Idaes* loue so deare:
Let father frowne and fret, and fret and die,
Nor earth, nor heauen shall part my loue and I.
Yea they shall part vs, but we first must meet,
And wo, and win, and yet the world not seet.
Yea ther's the wound, & wounded with thatthoght
So let me die: for all my drift is naught. 310

Ateu. Most gratious and imperiall Maiestie,

K. of S. A little flattery more were but too much,
Villaine what art thou that thus darest interrupt a Princes secrets.

Ateu. Dread King, thy vassall is a man of Art,
Who knowes by constellation of the stars,
By oppositions and by drie aspects,
The things are past, and those that are to come.

K. of S. But where's thy warrant to approach my presence?

Ateu. My zeale and ruth to see your graces wrong,
Makes me lament, I did detract so long. 320

K. of S. If thou knowst thoughts, tell me what mean I now?

Ateu. Ile calculate the cause of those your highnesse smiles,
And tell your thoughts.

K. of S. But least thou spend thy time in idlenesse,
And misse the matter that my mind aimes at,
Tell me what star was opposite when that was thought?

He strikes him on the eare.

Ateu. Tis inconuenient mightie Potentate,
Whose lookes resembles *Ioue* in Maiestie,
To scorne the sooth of science with contempt, 330
I see in those imperiall lookes of yours,
The whole discourse of loue, *Saturn* combust,
With direfull lookes at your natiuitie:
Beheld faire *Venns* in her siluerorbe,
I know by certaine exiomies I haue read,
Your graces griefs, & further can expresse her name,
That holds you thus in fancies bands.

K. of S. Thou talkest wonders.

Ateu. Nought but truth O King,
Tis *Ida* is the mistresse of your heart, 340
Whose youth must take impression of affects,
For tender twigs will bowe, and milder mindes
Will yeeld to fancie be they followed well.

K. of S. What god art thou composde in humane shape,
Or bold *Trophonius* to decide our doubts,
How knowst thou this?

Ateu. Euen as I know the meanes,
To worke your graces freedome and your loue:
Had I the mind as many Courtiers haue,
To creepe into your bosome for your coyne, 350
And beg rewards for euery cap and knee,
I then would say, if that your grace would giue
This lease, this manor, or this pattent seald,
For this or that I would effect your loue:
But *Ateukin* is no Parasite O Prince,
I know your grace knowes schollers are but poore,
And therefore as I blush to beg a fee,
Your mightinesse is so magnificent
You cannot chuse but cast some gift apart,
To ease my bashfull need that cannot beg, 360
As for your loue, oh might I be imployd,
How faithfully would *Ateukin* compasse it:
But Princes rather trust a smoothing tongue,
Then men of Art that can accept the time.

K. of Scots. Ateu. If so thy name, for so thou saist,
Thine Art appeares in entrance of my loue:
And since I deeme thy wisedom matcht with truth,
I will exalt thee, and thy selfe alone
Shalt be the Agent to dissolue my griefe.
Sooth is, I loue, and *Ida* is my loue, 370
But my new marriage nips me neare, *Ateukin*:
For *Dorithea* may not brooke th'abuse.

Ateu. These lets are but as moaths against the sun,
Yet not so great, like dust before the winde:
Yet not so light. Tut pacifie your grace,
You haue the sword and scepter in your hand,
You are the King, the state depends on you:
Your will is law, say that the case were mine,

Were she my sister whom your highnesse loues,
She should consent, for that our liues, our goods, 380
Depend on you, and if your Queene repine,
Although my nature cannot brooke of blood,
And Schollers grieue to heare of murtherous deeds,
But if the Lambe should let the Lyons way,
By my aduise the Lambe should lose her life.
Thus am I bold to speake vnto your grace,
Who am too base to kisse your royall feete,
For I am poore, nor haue I land nor rent,
Nor countenance here in Court, but for my loue,
Your Grace shall find none such within the realme. 390

    K. of S. Wilt thou effect my loue, shal she be mine?

    Ateu. Ile gather Moly-rocus, and the earbes,
That heales the wounds of body and the minde,
Ile set out charmes and spels, nought else shalbe left,
To tame the wanton if she shall rebell,
Giue me but tokens of your highnesse trust.

    K. of S.. Thou shalt haue gold, honor and wealth inough,
Winne my Loue, and I will make thee great.

    Ateu. These words do make me rich most noble Prince,
I am more proude of them then any wealth, 400
Did not your grace suppose I flatter you,
Beleeue me I would boldly publish this:
Was neuer eye that saw a sweeter face,
Nor neuer eare that heard a deeper wit,
Oh God how I am rauisht in your woorth.

    K. of S. Ateu. Follow me, loue must haue ease.

    Ateu. Ile kisse your highnesse feet, march when you please.

Exeunt.

Enter Slipper, Nano, *and* Andrew, *with their billes readie* I. ii.
written in their hands. 410

    Andrew. Stand back sir, mine shall stand highest.

    Slip. Come vnder mine arme sir, or get a footstoole,
Or else by the light of the Moone, I must come to it.

    Nano. Agree my maisters, euery man to his height,
Though I stand lowest, I hope to get the best maister.

Andr. Ere I will stoupe to a thistle, I will change turnes,
As good lucke comes on the right hand, as the left:
Here's for me, and me, and mine.

Andr. But tell me fellowes till better occasion come,
Do you seeke maisters? 420

Ambo. We doo.

Andr. But what can you do worthie preferment?

Nano. Marry I can smell a knaue from a Rat.

Slip. And I can licke a dish before a Cat.

Andr. And I can finde two fooles vnfought,
How like you that?
But in earnest, now tell me of what trades are you two?

Slip. How meane you that sir, of what trade?
Marry Ile tell you, I haue many trades,
The honest trade when I needs must, 430
The filching trade when time serues,
The Cousening trade as I finde occasion.
And I haue more qualities, I cannot abide a ful cup vnkist,
A fat Capon vncaru'd,
A full purse vnpickt,
Nor a foole to prooue a Iustice as you do.

Andr. Why sot why calst thou me foole?

Nano. For examining wiser then thy selfe.

Andr. So doth many more then I in *Scotland.*

Nano. Yea those are such, as haue more autthoritie then wit, 440
And more wealth then honestie.

Slip. This is my little brother with the great wit, ware him,
But what canst thou do, tel me, that art so inquisitiue of vs?

Andr. Any thing that concernes a gentleman to do, that can I do.

Slip. So you are of the gentle trade?

Andr. True.

Slip. Then gentle sir, leaue vs to our selues,
For heare comes one as if he would lack a seruant ere he went.
Ent. *Ateu.* Why so *Ateukin*? this becomes thee best,
Wealth, honour, ease, and angelles in thy chest: 450
Now may I say, as many often sing,

No fishing to the sea, nor seruice to a king.
Vnto this high promotions doth belong,
Meanes to be talkt of in the thickest throng:
And first to fit the humors of my Lord,
Sweete layes and lynes of loue I must record.
And such sweete lynes and louelayes ile endite:
As men may wish for, and my leech delight,
And next a traine of gallants at my heeles,
That men may say, the world doth run on wheeles. 460
For men of art, that rise by indirection,
To honour and the fauour of their King,
Must vse all meanes to saue what they haue got,
And win their fauours whom he neuer knew.
If any frowne to see my fortunes such,
A man must beare a little, not too much:
But in good time these billes partend, I thinke,
That some good fellowes do for seruice seeke.

Read. *If any gentleman, spirituall or temperall, will entertaine*
out of his seruice, a young stripling of the age of 30. yeares, that can 470
sleep with the soundest, eate with the hungriest, work with the sickest,
lye with the lowdest, face with the proudest, &c. that can wait in a
Gentlemans chamber, when his maister is a myle of, keepe his stable
when tis emptie, and his purse when tis full, and hath many qualities
woorse then all these, let him write his name and goe his way,
and attendance shall be giuen.

Ateu. By my faith a good seruant, which is he?

Slip. Trulie sir that am I?

Ateu. And why doest thou write such a bill,
Are all these qualities in thee? 480

Slip. O Lord I sir, and a great many more,
Some bettet, some worse, some richer some porer,
Why sir do you looke so, do they not please you?

Ateu. Trulie no, for they are naught and so art thou,
If thou hast no better qualities, stand by.

Slip. O sir, I tell the worst first, but and you lack a man,
I am for you, ile tell you the best qualities I haue.

Ateu. Be breefe then.

Slip. If you need me in your chamber,

14

I can keepe the doore at a whistle, in your kitchin, 490
Turne the spit, and licke the pan, and make the fire burne.
But if in the stable.

Ateu. Yea there would I vse thee.

Slip. Why there you kill me, there am I,
And turne me to a horse & a wench, and I haue no peere.

Ateu. Art thou so good in keeping a horse,
I pray thee tell me how many good qualities hath a horse?

Slip. Why so sir, a horse hath two properties of a man,
That is a proude heart, and a hardie stomacke,
Foure properties of a Lyon, a broad brest, a stiffe docket, 500
Hold your nose master. A wild countenance, and 4. good legs.
Nine properties of a Foxe, nine of a Hare, nine of an Asse,
And ten of a woman.

Ateu. A woman, why what properties of a woman hath a Horse?

Slip. O maister, know you not that?
Draw your tables, and write what wise I speake.
First a merry countenance.
Second, a soft pace.
Third, a broad forehead.
Fourth, broad buttockes. 510
Fift, hard of warde.
Sixt, easie to leape vpon.
Seuenth, good at long iourney.
Eight, mouing vnder a man.
Ninth, alway busie with the mouth.
Tenth. Euer chewing on the bridle.

Ateu. Thou art a man for me, whats thy name?

Slip. An auncient name sir, belonging to the
Chamber and the night gowne. Gesse you that.

Ateu. Whats that, *Slipper*? 520

Slip. By my faith well gest, and so tis indeed:
Youle be my maister?

Ateu. I meane so.

Slip. Reade this first.

Ateu. Pleaseth it any Gentleman to entertaine

A seruant of more wit then stature,
Let them subscribe, and attendance shall be giuen.
What of this?

Slip. He is my brother sir, and we two were borne togither,
Must serue togither, and will die togither, 530
Though we be both hangd.

Ateu. Whats thy name?

Nano. Nano.

Ateu. The etimologie of which word, is a dwarfe:
Art not thou the old stoykes son that dwels in his Tombe?

Ambo. We are.

Ateu. Thou art welcome to me,
Wilt thou giue thy selfe wholly to be at my disposition?

Nano. In all humilitie I submit my selfe.

Ateu. Then will I deck thee Princely, instruct thee courtly, 540
And present thee to the Queene as my gift.
Art thou content?

Nano. Yes, and thanke your honor too.

Slip. Then welcome brother, and fellow now.

Andr. May it please your honor to abase your eye so lowe,
As to looke either on my bill or my selfe.

Ateu. What are you?

An. By birth a gentleman, in profession a scholler,
And one that knew your honor in *Edenborough*,
Before your worthinesse cald you to this reputation. 550
                    By me *Andrew Snoord.*

Ateu. Andrew I remember thee, follow me,
And we will confer further, for my waightie affaires
For the king, commands me to be briefe at this time.
Come on *Nano, Slipper* follow.

                                            Exeunt.

Enter sir *Bartram* with *Eustas* and others, booted. *I. iii.*

S. Bar. But tell me louely *Eustas* as thou lou'st me,
Among the many pleasures we haue past,
Which is the rifest in thy memorie, 560

To draw thee ouer to thine auncient friend?

Eu. What makes Sir *Bartram* thus inquisitiue?
Tell me good knight, am I welcome or no?

Sir Bar. By sweet S. *Andrew* and may sale I sweare,
As welcom is my honest *Dick* to me,
As mornings sun, or as the watry moone,
In merkist night, when we the borders track.
I tell thee *Dick*, thy sight hath cleerd my thoughts,
Of many banefull troubles that there woond.
Welcome to sir *Bartram* as his life: 570
Tell me bonny *Dicke*, hast got a wife?

Eust. A wife God shield sir *Bartram*, that were ill
To leaue my wife and wander thus astray:
But time and good aduise ere many yeares,
May chance to make my fancie bend that way,
What newes in *Scotland*? therefore came I hither:
To see your Country, and to chat togither.

Sir Bar. Why man our Countries blyth, our king is well.
Our Queene so, so, the Nobles well, and worse
And weele are they that were about the king, 580
But better are the Country Gentlemen.
And I may tell thee *Eustace*, in our liues,
We old men neuer saw so wondrous change:
But leaue this trattle, and tell me what newes,
In louely England with our honest friends?

Eust. The king, the Court, and all our noble frends
Are well, and God in mercy keepe them so.
The Northren Lords and Ladies here abouts,
That knowes I came to see your Queen and Court,
Commends them to my honest friend sir *Bartram*, 590
And many others that I haue not seene:
Among the rest, the Countesse *Elinor* from *Carlile*
Where we merry oft haue bene,
Greets well my Lord, and hath directed me,
By message this faire Ladies face to see.

Sir Bar. I tell thee *Eustace*, lest mine old eyes daze,
This is our Scottish moone and euenings pride:
This is the blemish of your English Bride:
Who sailes by her, are sure of winde at will.
Her face is dangerous, her sight is ill: 600

17

And yet in sooth sweet *Dicke*, it may be said,
The king hath folly, their's vertue in the mayd.

Eust. But knows my friend this portrait, be aduisd?

Sir Bar. Is it not *Ida* the Countesse of *Arains* daughters?

Eust. So was I told by *Elinor* of *Carlile*,
But tell me louely *Bartram*, is the maid euil inclind,
Misled, or Concubine vnto the King or any other Lord?

Ba. Shuld I be brief & true, thē thus my *Dicke*,
All Englands grounds yeelds not a blyther Lasse.
Nor *Europ* can art her for her gifts, 610
Of vertue, honour, beautie, and the rest:
But our fōd king not knowing sin in lust,
Makes loue by endlesse meanes and precious gifts,
And men that see it dare not sayt my friend,
But wee may wish that it were otherwise:
But I rid thee to view the picture still,
For by the persons sights there hangs som ill.

Ba. Oh good sir *Bartram*, you suspect I loue,
Then were I mad, hee whom I neuer sawe,
But how so ere, I feare not entisings, 620
Desire will giue no place vnto a king:
Ile see her whom the world admires so much,
That I may say with them, there liues none such.

Bar. Be Gad and sal, both see and talke with her,
And when th' hast done, what ere her beautie be,
Ile wartant thee her vertues may compare,
With the proudest she that waits vpon your Queen.

Eu. My Ladie intreats your Worship in to supper.

Ba. Guid bony *Dick*, my wife will tel thee more,
Was neuer no man in her booke before: 630
Be Gad shees blyth, faire lewely, bony, &c.

Exeunt.

Enter Bohan *and the fairy king after the first act, to* II. Chor.
them a rownd of Fairies, or some prittie dance.

Boh. Be Gad gramersis little king for this,
This sport is better in my exile life,
Then euer the deceitfuil werld could yeeld.

Ober. I tell thee *Bohan*, *Oberon* is king,
Of quiet, pleasure, profit, and content,
Of wealth, of honor, and of all the world, 640
Tide to no place, yet all are tide to one,
Liue thou in this life, exilde from world and men,
And I will shew thee wonters ere we part,

Boh. Then marke my stay, and the strange doubts,
That follow flatterers, lust and lawlesse will,
And then say I haue reason to forsake the world,
And all that are within the same.
Gow shrowd vs in our harbor where weele see,
The pride of folly, as it ought to be.

Exeunt. 650

After the first act.

Ober. Here see I good fond actions in thy gyg,
And meanes to paint the worldes in constant waies
But turne thine ene, see which for I can commaund.

> *Enter two battailes strongly fighting, the one* Simi Ranus, *the other,* Staurobates, *she flies, and her Crowne is taken, and she hurt.*

Boh. What gars this din of mirk and balefull harme,
Where euery weane is all betaint with bloud?

Ober. This shewes thee *Bohan* what is worldly pompe. 660

Simeranu., the proud Assirrian Queene,
When *Ninus* died, did tene in her warres,
Three millions of footemen to the fight,
Fiue hundreth thousand horse, of armed chars,
A hundreth thousand more yet in her pride
Was hurt and conquered by *S. Taurobates.*
Then what is pompe?

Bohan. I see thou art thine ene.
Thou bonny King, if Princes fall from high,
My fall is past, vntill I fall to die. 670
Now marke my talke, and prosecute my gyg.

2.

Ober. How shuld these crafts withdraw thee from the world?
But looke my *Bohan*, pompe allureth.

19

Enter Cirus *king, humbling themselues: himselfe crowned by*
Oliue Pat, *at last dying, layde in a marbell tombe with this*
inscription

Who so thou bee that passest,
For I know one shall passe, knowe I
I am *Cirus* of *Persia*, 680
And I prithee leaue me not thus like a clod of clay
Wherewith my body is couered.

All exeunt.

Enter the king in great pompe, who reads it, & issueth,
crieth vermeum.

Boha. What meaneth this?

Ober. Cirus of *Persia,*
Mightie in life, within a marbell graue,
Was layde to rot, whom *Alexander* once
Beheld in tombde, and weeping did confesse 690
Nothing in life could scape from wrethednesse:
Why then boast men?

Boh. What recke I then of life,
Who makes the graue my tomb, the earth my wife:
But marke mee more.

3.

Boh. I can no more, my patience will not warpe.
To see these flatteries how they scorne and carpe.

Ober. Turne but thy head.

Enter our kings carring Crowns, Ladies presenting odors 700
to Potentates in thrond, who suddainly is slaine
by his seruaunts, and thrust out, and so they eate.

Exeunt.

Sike is the werld, but whilke is he I sawe.

Ober. Sesostris who was conquerour of the werld,
Slaine at the last, and stampt on by his slaues.

Boh. How blest are peur men then that know their graue,
Now marke the sequell of my Gig.

Boh. An he weele meete ends: the mirk and sable night
Doth leaue the pering morne to prie abroade,

20

Thou nill me stay, haile then thou pride of kings,
I ken the world, and wot well worldly things,
Marke thou my gyg, in mirkest termes that telles
The loathe of sinnes, and where corruption dwells
Haile me ne mere with showes of gudlie sights:
My graue is mine, that rids me from dispights.
Accept my gig guid King, and let me rest,
The graue with guid men, is a gay built nest.

 Ober. The rising sunne doth call me hence away,
Thankes for thy gyg, I may no longer stay: 720
But if my traine, did wake thee from thy rest,
So shall they sing, thy lullabie to nest.

   Actus Secundus. Schena Prima. II. i.

   *Enter the Countesse of Arrain, with Ida her daughter
   in theyr porch, sitting at worke.*

   A Song.

 Count. Faire *Ida*, might you chuse the greatest good
Midst all the world, in blessings that abound:
Wherein my daughter shuld your liking be?

 Ida. Not in delights, or pompe, or maiestie. 730

 Count. And why?

 Ida. Since these are meanes to draw the minde
From perfect good, and make true iudgement blind.

 Count. Might you haue wealth, and fortunes ritchest store?

 Ida. Yet would I (might I chuse) be honest poore.
For she that sits at fortunes feete alowe
Is sure she shall not taste a further woe.
But those that prancke one top of fortunes ball,
Still feare a change: and fearing catch a fall.

 Count. Tut foolish maide, each one contemneth need. 740

 Ida. Good reasõ why, they know not good indeed.

 Count. Many marrie then, on whom distresse doth loure,

 Ida. Yes they that vertue deeme an honest dowre.
Madame, by right this world I may compare,
Vnto my worke, wherein with heedfull care,
The heauenly workeman plants with curious hand,

21

As I with needle drawe each thing one land,
Euen as hee list, some men like to the Rose,
Are fashioned fresh, some in their stalkes do close,
And borne do suddaine die: some are but weeds, 750
And yet from them a secret good proceeds:
I with my needle if I please may blot,
The fairest rose within my cambricke plot,
God with a becke can change each worldly thing,
The poore to earth, the begger to the king.
What then hath man, wherein hee well may boast,
Since by a becke he liues, a louer is lost?

   Enter Eustace with letters.

 Count. Peace *Ida*, heere are straungers neare at hand.

 Eust. Madame God speed. 760

 Count. I thanke you gentle squire.

 Eust. The countrie Countesse of *Northumberland*,
Doth greete you well, and hath requested mee,
To bring these letters to your Ladiship.

   He carries the letter.

 Count. I thanke her honour, and your selfe my friend.

    Shee receiues and peruseth them.

I see she meanes you good braue Gentleman,
Daughter, the Ladie *Elinor* salutes
Your selfe as well as mee, then for her sake 770
T'were good you entertaind that Courtiour well.

 Ida. As much salute as may become my sex,
And hee in vertue can vouchsafe to thinke,
I yeeld him for the courteous Countesse sake.
Good sir sit downe, my mother heere and I,
Count time mispent, an endlesse vanitie.

 Eust. Beyond report, the wit, the faire, the shape,
What worke you heere, faire Mistresse may I see it?

 Id. Good Sir looke on, how like you this compact?

 Eust. Me thinks in this I see true loue in act: 780
The Woodbines with their leaues do sweetly spred,
The Roses blushing prancke them in their red,

22

No flower but boasts the beauties of the spring,
This bird hath life indeed if it could sing:
What meanes faire Mistres had you in this worke?

Ida. My needle sir.

Eust. In needles then there lurkes,
Some hidden grace I deeme beyond my reach.

Id. Not grace in thẽ good sir, but those that teach.

Eust. Say that your needle now were *Cupids* sting, 790
But ah her eie must bee no lesse,
In which is heauen and heauenlinesse,
In which the foode of God is shut,
Whose powers the purest mindes do glut.

Ida. What if it were?

Eust. Then see a wondrous thing,
I feare mee you would paint in *Teneus* heart,
Affection in his power and chiefest parts.

Ida. Good Lord sir no, for hearts but pricked soft,
Are wounded sore, for so I heare it oft. 800

Eust. what recks the second,
Where but your happy eye,
May make him liue, whom *Ioue* hath iudgd to die.

Ida. Should life & death within this needle lurke,
Ile pricke no hearts, Ile pricke vpon my worke.

Enter Ateuken, with Slipper the Clowne.

Coun. Peace *Ida*, I perceiue the fox at hand.

Eust. The fox? why fetch your hounds & chace him hence.

Count. Oh sir these great men barke at small offence.

Ateu. Come will it please you to enter gentle sir? 810

Offer to exeunt.

Stay courteous Ladies, fauour me so much,
As to discourse a word or two apart.

Count. Good sir, my daughter learnes this rule of mee,
To shun resort, and straungers companie:
For some are shifting mates that carrie letters,
Some such as you too good, because our betters.

Slip. Now I pray you sir what a kin are you to a pickrell?

Ateu. Why knaue?

Slip. By my troth sir, because I neuer knew a proper scituation[820] fellow of your pitch, fitter to swallow a gudgin.

Ateu. What meanst thou by this?

Slip. Shifting fellow sir, these be thy words, shifting fellow: This Gentlewoman I feare me, knew your bringing vp.

Ateu. How so?

Slip. Why sir your father was a Miller,
That could shift for a pecke of grist in a bushell,
And you a faire spoken Gentleman, that can get more land by
a lye, then an honest man by his readie mony.

Ateu. Catiue what sayest thou? [830]

Slip. I say sir, that if shee call you shifting knaue,
You shall not put her to the proofe.

Ateu. And why?

Slip. Because sir, liuing by your wit as you doo shifting, is your letters pattents, it were a hard matter for mee to get my dinner that day, wherein my Maister had not solde a dozen of deuices, a case of cogges, and a shute of shifts in the morning: I speak this in your commendation sir, & I pray you so take it.

Ateu. If I liue knaue I will bee reuenged, what Gentleman would entertaine a rascall, thus to derogate from his honour? [840]

Ida. My Lord why are you thus impatient?

Ateu. Not angrie *Ida*, but I teach this knaue,
How to behaue himselfe among his betters:
Behold faire Countesse to assure your stay,
I heere present the signet of the king,
Who now by mee faire *Ida* doth salute you:
And since in secret I haue certaine things,
In his behalfe good Madame to impart,
I craue your daughter to discourse a part.

Count. Shee shall in humble dutie bee addrest, [850]
To do his Highnesse will in what shee may.

Id. Now gentle sir what would his grace with me?

24

Ateu. Faire comely Nimph, the beautie of your face,
Sufficient to bewitch the heauenly powers,
Hath wrought so much in him, that now of late
Hee findes himselfe made captiue vnto loue,
And though his power and Maiestie requires,
A straight commaund before an humble sute,
Yet hee his mightinesse doth so abase,
As to intreat your fauour honest maid. 860

Ida. Is hee not married sir vnto our Queen?

Ateu. Hee is.

Ida. And are not they by God accurst,
That seuer them whom hee hath knit in one?

Ateu. They bee: what then? wee seeke not to displace
The Princesse from her seate, but since by loue
The king is made your owne, shee is resolude
In priuate to accept your dalliance,
In spight of warre, watch, or worldly eye.

Ida. Oh how hee talkes as if hee should not die, 870
As if that God in iustice once could winke,
Vpon that fault I am a sham'd to thinke.

Ateu. Tut Mistresse, man at first was born to erre,
Women are all not formed to bee Saints:
Tis impious for to kill our natiue king,
Whom by a little fauour wee may saue.

Ida. Better then liue vnchaste, to liue in graue.

Ateu. Hee shall erect your state & wed you well.

Ida. But can his warrant keep my soule from hell?

Ateu. He will inforce, if you resist his sute. 880

Id. What tho, the world may shame to him account
To bee a king of men and worldly pelfe.

Ateu. Yet hath to power no rule and guide himselfe,
I know you gentle Ladie and the care,
Both of your honour and his graces health,
Makes me confused in this daungerous state.

Ida. So counsell him, but sooth thou not his sinne,
Tis vaine alurement that doth make him loue,

25

I shame to heare, bee you a shamde to mooue.

Count. I see my daughter growes impatient, 890
I feare me hee pretends some bad intent.

Ateu. Will you dispise the king, & scorne him so?

Ida. In all alleageance I will serue his grace,
But not in lust, oh how I blush to name it?

Ateu. An endlesse worke is this, how should I frame it?

They discourse priuately.

Slip. Oh Mistresse may I turne a word vpon you.

Ateu. Friend what wilt thou?

Slip. Oh what a happie Gentlewoman bee you trulie, the
world reports this of you Mistresse, that a man can no sooner 900
come to your house, but the Butler comes with a blacke Iack
and sayes welcome friend, heeres a cup of the best for you, verilie
Mistresse you are said to haue the best Ale in al *Scotland*.

Count. Sirrha go fetch him drinke, how likest thou this?

Slip. Like it Mistresse? why this is quincy quarie pepper
de watchet, single goby, of all that euer I tasted: Ile prooue in
this Ale and tost, the compasse of the whole world. First this
is the earth, it ties in the middle a faire browne tost, a goodly
countrie for hungrie teeth to dwell vpon: next this is the sea,
a fair poole for a drie tõgue to fish in: now come I, & seing the 910
world is naught, I diuide it thus, & because the sea cãnot stand
without the earth, as *Arist.* saith, I put thẽ both into their first
Chaos which is my bellie, and so mistresse you may see your ale
is become a myracle.

Eustace. A merrie mate Madame I promise you.

Count. Why sigh you sirrah?

Slip. Trulie Madam, to think vppon the world, which since
I denoũced, it keepes such a rumbling in my stomack, that vnlesse
your Cooke giue it a counterbuffe with some of your rosted
Capons or beefe, I feare me I shal become a loose body, so 920
daintie I thinke, I shall neither hold fast before nor behinde.

Count. Go take him in and feast this merrie swaine,
Syrrha, my cooke is your phisitian.
He hath a purge for to disiest the world.

26

Ateu. Will you not, *Ida*, grant his highnesse this?

Ida. As I haue said, in dutie I am his:
For other lawlesse lusts, that ill beseeme him,
I cannot like, and good I will not deeme him.

Count. Ida come in, and sir if so you please,
Come take a homelie widdowes intertaine. 930

Ida. If he haue no great haste, he may come nye.
If haste, tho he be gone, I will not crie.

Exeunt.

Ateu. I see this labour lost, my hope in vaine,
Yet will I trie an other drift againe.

Enter the Bishop of S. Andrewes, Earle Douglas, II. ii.
Morton, with others, one way, the Queene with
Dwarfes an other way.

B. S. Andr. Oh wrack of Cõmon-weale! Oh wretched state!

Doug. Oh haplesse flocke whereas the guide is blinde? 940

They all are in a muse.

Mort. Oh heedlesse youth, where counsaile is dispis'd.

Dorot. Come prettie knaue, and prank it by my side,
Lets see your best attendaunce out of hande.

Dwarfe. Madame altho my lims are very small,
My heart is good, ile serue you therewithall.

Doro. How if I were assaild, what couldst thou do?

Dwarf. Madame call helpe, and boldly fight it to,
Altho a Bee be but a litle thing:
You know faire Queen, it hath a bitter sting. 950

Dor. How couldst thou do me good were I in greefe?

Dwar. Counsell deare Princes, is a choyce releefe.
Tho *Nestor* wanted force, great was his wit,
And tho I am but weake, my words are fit.

S. And. Like to a ship vpon the Ocean seas,
Tost in the doubtfull streame without a helme,
Such is a Monarke without good aduice,
I am ore heard, cast raine vpon thy tongue,
Andrewes beware, reproofe will breed a fear.

27

Mor. Good day my Lord. 960

B. S. And. Lord *Morton* well ymet:
Whereon deemes Lord *Douglas* all this while?

Dou. Of that which yours and my poore heart doth breake:
Altho feare shuts our mouths we dare not speake.

Dor. What meane these Princes sadly to consult?
Somewhat I feare, betideth them amisse,
They are so pale in lookes, so vext in minde:
In happie houre the Noble Scottish Peeres
Haue I incountred you, what makes you mourne?

B. S. And. If we with patience may attentiue gaine, 970
Your Grace shall know the cause of all our griefe.

Dor. Speake on good father, come and sit by me:
I know thy care is for the common good.

B. S. And. As fortune mightie Princes reareth some,
To high estate, and place in Common-weale,
So by diuine bequest to them is lent,
A riper iudgement and more searching eye:
Whereby they may discerne the common harme,
For where importunes in the world are most,
Where all our profits rise and still increase, 980
There is our minde, thereon we meditate,
And what we do partake of good aduice,
That we imploy for to concerne the same.)
To this intent these nobles and my selfe,
That are (or should bee) eyes of Common-weale,
Seeing his highnesse reachlesse course of youth
His lawlesse and vnbridled vaine in loue,
His to intentiue trust too flatterers,
His abiect care of councell and his friendes,
Cannot but greeue, and since we cannot drawe 990
His eye or Iudgement to discerne his faults
Since we haue spake and counsaile is not heard,
I for my part, (let others as they list)
Will leaue the Court, and leaue him to his will:
Least with a ruthfull eye I should behold,
His ouerthrow which sore I feare is nye.

Doro. Ah father are you so estranged from loue,
From due alleageance to your Prince and land,

To leaue your King when most he needs your help,
The thriftie husbandmen, are neuer woont 1000
That see their lands vnfruitfull, to forsake them:
But when the mould is barraine and vnapt,
They toyle, they plow, and make the fallow fatte:
The pilot in the dangerous seas is knowne,
In calmer waues the sillie sailor striues,
Are you not members Lords of Common-weale,
And can your head, your deere annointed King,
Default ye Lords, except your selues do faile?
Oh stay your steps, returne and counsaile him.

    Doug. Men seek not mosse vpon a rowling stone, 1010
Or water from the siue, or fire from yce:
Or comfort from a rechlesse monarkes hands.
Madame he sets vs light that seru'd in Court,
In place of credit in his fathers dayes,
If we but enter presence of his grace,
Our payment is a frowne, a scoffe, a frumpe,
Whilst flattering *Gnato* prancks it by his side,
Soothing the carelesse King in his misdeeds,
And if your grace consider your estate,
His life should vrge you too if all be true. 1020

    Doug. Why *Douglas* why?

    Doug. As if you haue not heard
His lawlesse loue to *Ida* growne of late,
His carelesse estimate of your estate.

    Doro. Ah *Douglas* thou misconstrest his intent,
He doth but tempt his wife, he tryees my loue:
This iniurie pertaines to me, not to you.
The King is young, and if he step awrie,
He may amend, and I will loue him still.
Should we disdaine our vines becauso they sprout 1030
Before their time? or young men if they straine
Beyõd their reach? no vines that bloome and spread
Do promise fruites, and young men that are wilde,
In age growe wise, my freendes and Scottish Peeres,
If that an English Princesse may preuaile,
Stay, stay with him, lo how my zealous prayer
Is plead with teares, fie Peeres will you hence?

    S. And. Madam tis vertue in your grace to plead,

But we that see his vaine vntoward course,
Cannot but flie the fire before it burne, 1040
And shun the Court before we see his fall.

Doro. Wil you not stay? then Lordings fare you well.
Tho you forsake your King, the heauens I hope
Will fauour him through mine incessant prayer.

Dwar. Content you Madam, thus old *Ouid* sings.
Tis foolish to bewaile recurelesse things.

Dorothea. Peace Dwarffe, these words my patience moue.

Dwar. All tho you charme my speech, charme not my loue

Exeunt Nano Dorothea.

Enter the King of Scots, Arius, the nobles spying 1050
him, returnes.

K. of S. Douglas how now? why changest thou thy cheere?

Dougl. My priuate troubles are so great my liege,
As I must craue your licence for a while:
For to intend mine owne affaires at home.   *Exit.*

King. You may depart, but why is *Morton* sad?

Mor. The like occasion doth import me too,
So I desire your grace to giue me leaue.

K. of S. Well sir you may betake you to your ease,
When such grim syrs are gone, I see no let 1060
To worke my will.

8. Atten. What like the Eagle then,
With often flight wilt thou thy feathers loose?
O King canst thou indure to see thy Court,
Of finest wits and Iudgements dispossest,
Whilst cloking craft with soothing climbes so high,
As each bewailes ambition is so bad?
Thy father left thee with estate and Crowne,
A learned councell to direct thy Court,
These careleslie O King thou castest off, 1070
To entertaine a traine of Sicophants:
Thou well mai'st see, although thou wilt not see,
That euery eye and eare both sees and heares
The certaine signes of thine inconstinence:
Thou art alyed vnto the English King,

30

By marriage a happie friend indeed,
If vsed well, if not a mightie foe.
Thinketh your grace he ean indure and brooke,
To haue a partner in his daughters loue?
Thinketh your grace the grudge of priuie wrongs 1080
Will not procure him chaunge his smiles to threats?
Oh be not blinde to good, call home your Lordes,
Displace these flattering Gnatoes, driue them hence:
Loue and with kindnesse take your wedlocke wife
Or else (which God forbid) I feare a change,
Sinne cannot thriue in courts without a plague.

K. of S. Go pack thou too, vnles thou mēd thy talk:
On paine of death proud Bishop get you gone,
Vnlesse you headlesse mean to hoppe away.

8. *Atten.* Thou god of heauē preuent my countries fall. 1090

Exeunt.

K. of S. These staies and lets to pleasure, plague my thoughts,
Forcing my greeuous wounds a new to bleed:
Bur care that hath transported me so farre,
Faire *Ida* is disperst in thought of thee:
Whose answere yeeldes me life, or breeds my death:
Yond comes the messenger of weale or woe.

Enter Gnato.

Ateuki. What newes?

Ateu. The adament o King will not be filde, 1100
But by it selfe, and beautie that exceeds,
By some exeeding fauour must be wrought,
Ida is coy as yet, and doth repine,
Obiecting marriage, honour, feare, and death,
Shee's holy, wise, and too precise for me.

K. of S. Are these thy fruites of wits, thy sight in Art?
Thine eloquence? thy pollicie? thy drift?
To mocke thy Prince, thē catiue packe thee hence,
And let me die deuoured in my loue.

Ateu. Good Lord how rage gainsayeth reasons power, 1110
My deare, my gracious, and beloued Prince,
The essence of my sute, my God on earth,
Sit downe and rest your selfe, appease your wrath,

31

Least with a frowne yee wound me to the death:
Oh that I were included in my graue,
That eyther now to saue my Princes life,
Must counsell crueltie, or loose my King.

    K. of S. Why sirrha, is there meanes to mooue her minde?

    Ateu. Oh should I not offend my royall liege.

    K. of S. Tell all, spare nought, so I may gaine my loue. 1120

    Ateu. Alasse my soule why art thou torne in twaine,
For feare thou talke a thing that should displease?

    K. of S. Tut, speake what so thou wilt I pardon thee.

    Ateu. How kinde a word, how courteous is his grace:
Who would not die to succour such a king?
My liege, this louely mayde of modest minde,
Could well incline to loue, but that shee feares,
Faire *Dorotheas* power, your grace doth know,
Your wedlocke is a mightie let to loue:
Were *Ida* sure to bee your wedded wife, 1130
That then the twig would bowe, you might command.
Ladies loue, presents pompe and high estate.

    K. of S. Ah *Ateukin*, how shuld we display this let?

    Ateu. Tut mightie Prince, oh that I might bee whist.

    K. of S. Why dalliest thou?

    Ateu. I will not mooue my Prince,
I will preferre his safetie before my life:
Heare mee ô king, tis *Dorotheas* death,
Must do you good.

    K. of S. What, murther of my Queene? 1140
Yet to enioy my loue, what is my Queene?
Oh but my vowe and promise to my Queene:
I but my hope to gaine a fairer Queene,
With how contrarious thoughts am I withdrawne?
Why linger I twixt hope and doubtfull feare:
If *Dorothe* die, will *Ida* loue?

    Ateu. Shee will my Lord.

    K. of S. Then let her die.
Deuise, aduise the meanes,
Al likes me wel that lends me hope in loue. 1150

Ateu. What will your grace consent, then let mee worke:
Theres heere in Court a Frenchman *Iaques* calde,
A fit performer of our enterprise,
Whom I by gifts and promise will corrupt,
To slaye the Queene, so that your grace will seale
A warrant for the man to saue his life.

K. of S. Nought shall he want, write thou and I wil signe
And gentle *Gnato*, if my *Ida* yeelde,
Thon shalt haue what thou wilt, Ile giue the straight,
A Barrony, an Earledome for reward. 1160

Ateu. Frolicke young king, the Lasse shall bee your owne,
Ile make her blyth and wanton by my wit.

                                               Exennt.

Enter Bohan with Obiron. III. Chor.

3. *Act.*

Boh. So *Oberon*, now it beginnes to worke in kinde,
The aunceint Lords by leauing him aliue,
Disliking of his humors and respight,
Lets him run headlong till his flatterers,
Sweeting his thoughts of lucklesse lust, 1170
With vile perswations and alluring words,
Makes him make way by murther to his will,
Iudge fairie king, hast heard a greater ill?

Ober. Nor send more vertue in a countrie mayd,
I tell the *Bohan* it doth make me merrie,
To thinke the deeds the king meanes to performe.

Boha. To change that humour stand and see the rest,
I trow my sonne *Slipper* will shewes a iest.

    Enter Slipper with a companion, bog, or wench, dauncing a
    hornpipe, and daunce out againe. 1180

Boha. Now after this beguiling of our thoughts,
And changing them from sad to better glee,
Lets to our sell, and sit and see thee rest,
For I beleeue this Iig will prooue no iest.   *Exeunt.*

    Chorus Actus 3. Schena Prima. III. i.

    Enter Slipper one way, and S. Bartram another way.

Bar. Ho fellow, stay and let me speake with thee.

Sli. Fellow, frend thou doest disbuse me, I am a Gentlemã.

Bar. A Gentleman, how so?

Slip. Why I rub horses sir. 1190

Bar. And what of that?

Sip. Oh simple witted, marke my reason, they that do good
seruice in the Common-weale are Gentlemen, but such as rub
horses do good seruice in the Common-weale, Ergo tarbox
Maister Courtier, a Horse-keeper is a Gentleman.

Bar. Heere is ouermuch wit in good earnest:
But sirrha where is thy Maister?

Slip. Neither aboue ground nor vnder ground,
Drawing out red into white,
Swallowing that downe without chawing, 1200
That was neuer made without treading.

Bar. Why where is hee then?

Slip. Why in his seller, drinking a cup of neate and briske
claret, in a boule of siluer: Oh sir the wine runnes trillill down
his throat, which cost the poore viutnerd many a stampe before
it was made: but I must hence sir, I haue haste.

Bar. Why whither now I prithee?

Slip. Faith sir, to Sir *Siluester* a Knight hard by, vppon my
Maisters arrand, whom I must certifie this, that the lease of
Est Spring shall bee confirmed, and therefore must I bid him 1210
prouide trash, for my Maister is no friend without mony.

Bar. This is the thing for which I sued so long,
This is the lease which I by *Guatoes* meanes,
Sought to possesse by pattent from the King:
But hee iniurious man, who liues by crafts,
And selles kings fauours for who will giue most,
Hath taken bribes of mee, yet couertly
Will sell away the thing pertaines to mee:
But I haue found a present helpe I hope,
For to preuent his purpose and deceit: 1220
Stay gentle friend.

Slip. A good word, thou haste won me,
This word is like a warme candle to a colde stomacke.

Bar. Sirra wilt thou for mony and reward,
Conuay me certaine letters out of hand,
From out thy maisters pocket.

Slip. Will I sir, why, were it to rob my father, hang
my mother, or any such like trifles, I am at your
commaundement sir, what will you giue me sir?

S. Bar. A hundreth pounds. 1230

Slip. I am your man, giue me earnest, I am dead at a pocket
sir, why I am a lifter maister, by my occupation.

S. Bar. A lifter, what is that?

Slip. Why sir, I can lift a pot as well as any man, and picke a purse assoone as any theefe in my countrie.

S. Bar. Why fellow hold, heere is earnest,
Ten pound to assure thee, go dispatch,
And bring it me to yonder Tauerne thou seest,
And assure thy selfe thou shalt both haue
Thy skin full of wine, and the rest of thy mony. 1240

Slip. I will sir. Now roome for a Gentleman, my maisters,
who giues mee mony for a faire new Angell, a trimme new
Angell?

Exeunt.

Enter Andrew and Purueyer. III. ii.

Pur. Sirrha, I must needes haue your maisters horses,
The king cannot bee vnserued.

And. Sirrha you must needs go without them,
Because my Maister must be serued.

Pur. Why I am the kings Purueyer, 1250
And I tell thee I will haue them.

And. I am *Ateukins* seruant, Signior *Andrew*,
And I say thou shalt not haue them.

Pur. Heeres my ticket, denie it if thou darst.

And. There is the stable, fetch them out if thou darst.

Pur. Sirrha, sirrha, tame your tongue, least I make you.

And. Sirrha, sirrha, hold your hand, least I bum you.

Pur. I tell thee, thy Maisters geldings are good,
And therefore fit for the king.

An. I tell thee, my Maisters horses haue gald backes, 1260
And therefore cannot fit the King.
Purueyr, Purueyer, puruey thee of more wit, darst thou presume
to wrong my Lord *Ateukins*, being the chiefest man in
Court.

Pur. The more vnhappie Common-weale,
Where flatterers are chiefe in Court.

And. What sayest thou?

Pur. I say thon art too presumptuous,
And the officers shall schoole thee.

And. A figge for them and thee Purueyer, 1270
They seeke a knot in a ring, that would wrong
My maister or his seruants in this Court.

    Enter Iaques.

Pur. The world is at a wise passe,
When Nobilitie is a fraid of a flatterer.

Iaq. Sirrha, what be you that parley, contra Monsieur my
Lord *Ateukin, en bonne foy,* prate you against syr *Altesse,* mee
maka your test to leap from your shoulders, per ma foy cy fere
ie.

And. Oh signior Captaine, you shewe your selfe a forward 1280
and friendly Gentleman in my Maisters behalfe, I will cause
him to thanke you.

Iaq. Poultron speake me one parola against my bon Gentilhome,
I shal estrampe your guttes, and thumpe your backa,
that you no poynt mannage this tenne ours.

Pur. Sirrha come open me the stable,
And let mee haue the horses:
And fellow, for all your French bragges I will doo my dutie.

And. Ile make garters of thy guttes,
Thou villaine if thou enter this office. 1290

Iaq. Mort lieu, take me that cappa
Pour nostre labeur, be gonne villein in the mort.

Pur. What will you resist mee then?
Well the Councell fellow, Shall know of your insolency.

                    Exit.

Andr. Tell them what thou wilt, and eate that I can best
spare from my backe partes, and get you gone with a vengeance.

            Enter Gnato.

Ateu. Andrew. 1300

Andr. Sir.

Ateu. Where be my writings I put in my pocket last night.

Andr. Which sir, your annoations vpon Matchauell?

Ateu. No sir, the letters pattents for east spring.

An. Why sir you talk wonders to me, if you ask that questiõ.

Ateu. Yea sir, and wil work wonders too, which you vnlesse you finde them out, villaine search me them out and bring thẽ me, or thou art but dead.

Andr. A terrible word in the latter end of a sessions. Master were you in your right wits yesternight? 1310

Ateu. Doest thou doubt it?

Andr. I and why not sir, for the greatest Clarkes are not the wisest, and a foole may dance in a hood, as wel as a wise man in a bare frock: besides such as giue themselues to *Plulantia*, as you do maister, are so cholericke of complection, that that which they burne in fire ouer night, they seeke for with furie the next morning. Ah I take care of your worship, this common-weale should haue a great losse of so good a member as you are.

Ateu. Thou flatterest me. 1320

Andr. Is it flatterie in me sir to speake you faire?
What is it then in you to dallie with the King?

Ateu. Are you prating knaue,
I will teach you bettet nurture?
Is this the care you haue of my wardrop?
Of my accounts, and matters of trust?

Andr. Why alasse sir, in times past your garments haue beene so well inhabited, as your Tenants woulde giue no place to a Moathe to mangle them, but since you are growne greater and your Garments more fine and gaye, 1330 if your garments are not fit for hospitallitie, blame your pride, and commend my cleanlinesse: as for yout writings, I am not for them, nor they for mee.

Ateu. Villaine go, flie, finde them out:
If thou loosest them, thou loosest my credit.

And. Alasse sir? can I loose that you neuer had.

Ateu. Say you so, then hold feel you that you neuer felt.

Ia. Oh Monsieur, aies patient, pardon your pouure vallet,
Me bee at your commaundement.

Ateu. Signior *Iaques* wel met, you shall commaund me, 1340
Sirra go cause my writings be proclamed in the Market place,

Promise a great reward to them that findes them,
Looke where I supt and euery where.

   And. I will sir, now are two knaues well met, and three well
parted, if you conceiue mine enigma, Gentlemen what shal I
bee then, faith a plaine harpe shilling.   *Exeunt.*

   Ateu. Sieur Iaques, this our happy meeting hides,
Your friends and me, of care and greeuous toyle,
For I that looke into deserts of men,
And see among the souldiers in this court, 1350
A noble forward minde, and iudge thereof,
Cannot but seeke the meanes to raise them vp:
Who merrit credite in the Common-weale.
To this intent friend *Iaque* I haue found
A meanes to make you great, and well esteemd,
Both with the king, and with the best in Court:
For I espie in you a valiant minde,
Which makes mee loue, admire, and honour you:
To this intent (if so your trust and faith,
Your secrecie be equall with your force) 1360
I will impart a seruice to thy selfe,
Which if thou doest effect, the King, my selfe,
And what or hee, and I with him can worke,
Shall be imployd in what thou wilt desire.

   Iaq. Me sweara by my ten bones, my singniar, to be loyal to
your Lordships intents, affaires, ye my monsignieur, *qui non
fera ic pour.* Yea pleasure?
By my sworda me be no babie Lords.

   Ateu. Then hoping one thy truth, I prithe see,
How kinde *Ateukin* is to forward mee, 1370
Hold take this earnest pennie of my loue.
And marke my words, the King by me requires,
No slender seruice *Iaques* at thy hands.
Thou must by priuie practise make a way,
The Queene faire *Dorethea* as she sleepes:
Or how thou wilt, so she be done to death:
Thou shalt not want promotion heare in Court.

   Iaq. Stabba the woman, per ma foy, monsignieur, me thrusta
my weapon into her belle, so me may be gard per le roy.
Mee de your seruice. 1380
But me no be hanged pur my labor.

Ateu. Thou shalt haue warrant *Iaques* from the King,
None shall outface, gainsay and wrong my friend.
Do not I loue thee *Iaques*? feare not then,
I tell thee who so toucheth thee in ought,
Shall iniure me, I loue, I tender thee:
Thou art a subiect fit to serue his grace,
Iaques, I had a written warrant once,
But that by great misfortune late is lost,
Come wend we to S. *Andrewes*, where his grace 1390
Is now in progresse, where he shall assure
Thy safetie, and confirme thee to the act.

Iaques. We will attend your noblenesse.

Exeunt.

Enter Sir Bartram, Dorothea, the Queene, III. iii.
Nano, Lord Ross. Ladies
attendants.

Doro. Thy credite *Bartram* in the Scottish Court,,
Thy reuerend yeares, the stricknesse of thy vowes,
All these are meanes sufficient to perswade, 1400
But loue the faithfull lincke of loyall hearts,
That hath possession of my constant minde,
Exiles all dread, subdueth vaine supect,
Me thinks no craft should harbour in that brest,
Where Maiestie and vertue is mstaled:
Me thinke my beautie should not cause my death.

Bar. How gladly soueraigne Princesse would Ierre,
And binde my shame to saue your royall life:
Tis Princely in your selfe to thinke the best,
To hope his grace is guiltlesse of this crime, 1410
But if in due preuention you default,
How blinde are you that were forwarnd before.

Doro. Suspition without cause deserueth blame.

Bar. Who sees, and shunne not harmes, deserue the same:
Beholde the tenor of this traiterous plot.

Doro. What should I reade? Perhappes he wrote it not.

Bar. Heere is his warrant vnder seale and signe,
To *Iaques* borne in *France* to murther you.

Doro. Ah carelesse King, would God this were not thine
What tho I reade? Ah should I thinke it true? 1420

Rosse. The hand and seale confirmes the deede is his.

Doro. What know I tho, if now he thinketh this?

Nauo. Madame *Lucretius* faith, that to repent,
Is shildish wisdome to preuent.

Doro. What tho?

Nano. Then cease your teares, that haue dismaid you,
And crosse the foe before hee haue betrayed you.

Bar. What needes this long suggestions in this cause?
When euery circumstance confirmeth trueth:
First let the hidden mercie from aboue, 1430
Confirme your grace, since by a wondrous meanes,
The practise of your daungers came to light:
Next let the tokens of appooued trueth,
Gouerne and stay your thoughts, too much seduc't,
And marke the sooth, and listen the intent,
Your highnesse knowes, and these my nobleLords,
Can witnesse this, that whilest your husbands sirre
In happie peace possest the Scottish Crowne,
I was his sworne attendant heere in Court,
In daungerous sight I neuer fail'd my Lord. 1440
And since his death, and this your husbands raigne,
No labour, dutie, haue I left vndone,
To testifie my zeale vnto the Crowne:
But now my limmes are weake, mine eyes are dim,
Mine age vnweldie and vnmeete for toyle:
I came to court in hope for seruice past,
To gaine some lease to keepe me beeingolde,
There found I all was vpsie turuy turnd,
My friends displac'ff, the Nobles loth to craue,
Then fought I to the minion of the King, 1450
Auteukin, who allured by a bribe,
Assur'd me of the lease for which I fought:
But see the craft, when he had got the graunt,
He wrought to sell it to Sir *Siluester*,
In hope of greater earnings from his hands:
In briefe, I learnt his craft, and wrought the meanes,
By one his needie seruants for reward,
To steale from out his pocket all the briefes,

Which hee perform'd, and with reward resignd
Them when I read (now marke the power of God) 1460
I found this warrant seald among the rest,
To kill your grace, whom God long keepe aliue.
Thus in effect, by wonder are you sau'd,
Trifle not then, bnt seeke a speakie flight,
God will conduct your steppes, and shield the right.

   Dor. What should I do, ah poore vnhappy Queen?
Borne to indure what fortune cancontaine,
Ah lasse the deed is too apparant now:
But oh mine eyes were you as bent to hide,
As my poore heart is forward to forgiue. 1470
Ah cruell king, my loue would thee acquite,
Oh what auailes to be allied and matcht
With high estates that marry but in shewe?
Were I baser borne, my meane estate
Could warrant me from this impendent harme,
But to be great and happie these are twaine.
Ah *Rosse* what shall I do, how shall I worke?

   Rosse. With speedie letters to your father send,
Who will reuenge you, and defend your right.

   Dor. As if they kill not me, who with him fight? 1480
As if his brest be toucht, I am not wounded,
As if he waild, my ioyes were not confounded:
We are one heart, tho rent by hate in twaine:
One soule, one essence doth our weale containe:
What then can conquer him that kils not me?

   Rosse. If this aduice displease, then Madame flee.

   Dor. Where may I wend or trauel without feare?

   Na. Where not, in changing this attire you weare?

   Dor. What shall I clad me like a Country maide?

   Na. The pollicie is base I am affraide. 1490

   Dor. Why *Nano*?

   Na. Aske you why? what may a Queene
March foorth in homely weede and be not seene?
The Rose although in thornie shrubs she spread:
Is still the Rose, her beauties waxe not dead.
And noble mindes altho the coate be bare,

Are by their semblance knowne, how great they are

Bar. The Dwarfe saith true.

Dor. What garments likste thou than?

Na. Such as may make you seeme a proper man. 1500

Dor. He makes me blush and smile, tho I am sad.

Na. The meanest coat for safetie is not bad.

Dor. What shall I iet in breeches like a squire?
Alasse poore dwarfe, thy Mistresle is vnmeete.

Na. Tut, go me thus, your cloake before your face,
Your sword vpreard with queint & comely grace,
If any come and question what you bee,
Say you a man, and call for witnesse mee.

Dor. What should I weare a sword, to what intent?

Na. Madame for shewe, it is an ornament, 1510
If any wrong you, drawe a shining blade
Withdrawes a coward theese that would inuade.

Dor. But if I strike, and hee should strike againe,
What should I do? I feare I should bee slaine.

Nano. No, take it single on your dagger so,
Ile teach you Madame how to ward a blow.

Do. How litle shapes much substance may include?
Sir *Bartram*, *Rosse*, yee Ladies and my friends,
Since presence yeelds me death, and absence life,
Hence will I flie disguised like a squire, 1520
As one that seekes to liue in Itish warres,
You gentle *Rosse*, shal furnish my depart.

Ross. Yea Prince, & die with you with all my hart,
Vouchsafe me then in all extreamest states,
To waight on you and serue you with my best.

Dor. To me pertaines the woe, liue then in rest:
Friends fare you well, keepe secret my depart,
Nano alone shall my attendant bee.

Nan. Then Madame are you mand, I warrant ye,
Giue me a sword, and if there grow debate, 1530
Ile come behinde, and breake your enemies pate.

43

Ross. How sore wee greeue to part so soone away.

Dor. Greeue not for those that perish if they stay.

Nano. The time in words mispent, is litle woorth,
Madam walke on, and let them bring vs foorth.

Exeunt.

Chorus. *IV. Chor.*

Ent. Boha. So these sad motions makes the faire sleepe,
And sleep hee shall in quiet and content,
For it would make a marbell melt and weepe 1540
To see these treasons gainst the innocent:
But since shee scapes by flight to saue her life,
The king may chance repent she was his wife:
The rest is ruthfull, yet to beguilde the time,
Tis interlast with merriment and rime.

Exeuut.

Actus Quartus. Schena Prima. IV. i.

*After a noyse of hornes and showtings, enter certaine
Huntsmen, if you please, singing one way: another
way Ateukin and Iaques, Gnato.* 1550

Ateu. Say Gentlemen, where may wee finde the king?

Hunts. Euen heere at hand on hunting.
And at this houre hee taken hath a stand,
To kill a Deere.

Ateu. A pleasant worke in hand,
Follow your sport, and we will seeke his grace.

Hunts. When such him seeke, it is a wofull case.

*Exeunt Huntsman one way, Ateu. and Iaq. another,
Enter Eustace, Ida, and the Countesse. IV. ii.*

Count. Lord *Eustace*, as your youth & vertuous life, 1560
Deserues a faire, more faire and richer wife,
So since I am a mother, and do wit
What wedlocke is, and that which longs to it,
Before I meane my daughter to bestow,
Twere meete that she and I your state did know.

Eust. Madame if I consider *Idas* woorth,
I know my portions merrit none so faire,

44

And yet I hold in farme and yearly rent,
A thousand pound, which may her state content.

   Count. But what estate my Lord shall she possesse? 1570

   Eust. All that is mine, graue Countesse & no lesse.
But *Ida* will you loue?

   Ida. I cannot hate.

   Eust. But will you wedde?

   Ida. Tis Greeke to mee my Lord,
Ile wish you well, and thereon take my word.

   Eus.. Shall I some signe of fauour then receiue?

   Ida. I, if her Ladiship will giue me leaue.

   Count. Do what thou wilt.

   Ida. Then noble English Peere, 1580
Accept this ring, wherein my heart is set,
A constant heart, with burning flames befret:
But vnder written this: *O morte dura*:
Heereon when so you looke with eyes *Pura*,
The maide you fancie most will fauour you.

   Eust. Ile trie this heart, in hope to finde it true.

   Enter certaine Huntsmen and ladies.

   Hunts. Widdowe Countesse well ymet,
Euer may thy ioyes bee many,
Gentle *Ida* faire beset, 1590
Faire and wise, not fairer any:
Frolike Huntsmen of the game,
Willes you well, and giues you greeting.

   Ida. Thanks good Woodman for the same,
And our sport and merrie meeting.

   Hunts. Vnto thee we do present,
Siluer heart with arrow wounded.

   Eust. This doth shadow my lament,
Both feare and loue confounded.

   Ladies. To the mother of the mayde, 1600
Faire as th'lillies, red as roses,
Euen so many goods are saide,

45

As her selfe in heart supposes.

Count. What are you friends, that thus doth wish vs wel?

Hunts. Your neighbours nigh, that haue on hunting beene,
Who vnderstanding of your walking foorth,
Prepare this traine to entertaine you with,
This Ladie *Douglas*, this Sir *Egmond* is.

Count. Welcome ye Ladies, and thousand thanks for this,
Come enter you a homely widdowes house,   1610
And if mine entertainment please you let vs feast.

Hunts. A louely ladie neuer wants a guest.

Exeunt Manet, Eustace, Ida.

Eust. Stay gentle *Ida*, tell me what you deeme,
What doth this hast, this tender heart beseeme?

Ida. Why not my Lord, since nature teacheth art,
To sencelesse beastes to cure their greeuous smart.
Dictanum serues to close the wound againe.

Eust. What helpe for those that loue?

Ida. Why loue againe.   1620

Eust. Were I the Hart,

Ida. Then I the hearbe would bee.
You shall not die for help, come follow me.

Exeunt.

Enter Andrew and Iaques. IV. iii.

Iaq. Mon Deiu, what *malheure* be this, me come a the chamber,
Signior *Andrew, Mon Deiu,* taka my *poinyard en mon maine,*
to giue the *Estocade* to the *Damoisella, per ma foy, there was
no person, elle cest en alle.*

And. The woorse lucke *Iaques,* but because I am thy friend 1630
I will aduise the somewhat towards the attainement of the
gallowes.

Iaq. Gallowes, what be that?

An. Marrie sir, a place of great promotion, where thou shalt
by one turne aboue ground, rid the world of a knaue, & make
a goodly ensample for all bloodie villaines of thy profession.

46

Que ditte vous, Monsieur Andrew?

And. I say *Iaques*, thou must keep this path, and high thee,
for the Q. as I am certified, is departed with her dwarfe, apparelled
like a squire, ouertake her Frenchman, stab her, Ile 1640
promise thee this dubblet shall be happy.

Iaq. Purquoy?

And. It shall serue a iolle Gentleman,
Sir *Dominus Monsignior* Hangman.

Iaq. Cest tout, vn me will *rama pour le monoy.*

And. Go, and the rot consume thee? Oh what a trim world
is this? My maister lius by cousoning the king, I by fllattering
him: *Slipper* my fellow by stealing: and I by lying: is not this
a wylie accord, Gentlemen. This last night our iolly horsekeeper
beeing well stept in licor, confessed to me the stealing of
my Maisters writings, and his great reward: now dare I not 1650
bewraye him, least he discouer my knauerie, but thus haue I
wrought: I vnderstand he will passe this way, to prouide him
necessaries, but if I and my fellowes faile not, wee will teach
him such a lesson, as shall cost him a chiefe place on pennilesse
bench for his labour: but yond he comes.

Enter Slipper with a Tailor, a Shoomaker, and a Cutler.

Slip. Taylor.　　*Tayl.* Sir.

Slip. Let my dubblet bee white Northren, fiue groates the
yard, I tell thee I will bee braue.

Tayl. It shall sir. 1660

Slip. Now sir, cut it me like the battlements of a Custerd,
ful of round holes: edge me the sleeues with Couentry-blew,
and let the lynings bee of tenpenny locorum.

Tayl. Very good sir.

Slip. Make it the amorous cut, a flappe before.

Tayl. And why so? that fashion is stale.

Slip. Oh friend, thou art a simple fellow, I tell thee, a flap is
a great friend to a storrie, it stands him in stead of cleane napery,
and if a mans shert bee torne, it is a present penthouse to

47

defend him from a cleane huswifes scoffe. 1670

Tay. You say sooth sir.

Slip. Holde take thy mony, there is seuen shillings for the dubblet, and eight for the breeches, seuen and eight, birladie thirtie sixe is a faire deale of mony.

Tayl. Farwell sir.

Slip. Nay but stay Taylor.

Tayl. Why sir?

Slipper. Forget not this speciall mate,
Let my back parts bee well linde,
For there come many winter stormes from a windie bellie, 1680
I tell thee Shoo-maker.

Shoe-ma. Gentleman what shoo will it please you to haue?

Slip. A fine neate calues leather my friend.

Shoo. Oh sir, that is too thin, it will not last you.

Slip. I tell thee, it is my neer kinsman, for I am *Slipper*, which
hath his best grace in summer to bee suted in lakus skins,
Guidwife Clarke was my Grandmother, and Goodman Neatherleather
mine Vnckle, but my mother good woman. Alas,
she was a Spaniard, and being wel tande and drest by a good-fellow,
an Englishman, is growne to some wealth: as when I 1690
haue but my vpper parts, clad in her husbands costlie Spannish
leather, I may bee bold to kisse the fayrest Ladies foote
in this contrey.

Shoo. You are of high birth sir,
But haue you all your mothers markes on you?

Slip. Why knaue?

Shoomaker. Because if thou come of the bloud of the *Slippers*,
you should haue a Shoomakers Alle thrust through your
eare.

Exit. 1700

Slip. Take your earnest friend and be packing,
And meddle not with my progenators *Cutler.*

Cutler. Heare sir.

Slip. I must haue a Rapier and Dagger.

Cutler. A Rapier and Dagger you meane sir?

Slipper. Thou saiest true, but it must haue a verie faire edge,

Cutler. Why so sir?

Slip. Because it may cut by himselfe, for trulie my freende,
I am a man of peace, and weare weapons but for facion.

Cutler. Well sir, giue me earnest I will fit you. |1710|

Slip. Hold take it, I betrust thee friend, let me be wel armed.

Cutler. You shall.   *Exit Cutler.*

Slip. Nowe what remaines? theres twentie Crownes for a
house, three crownes for houshol stuffe, six pence to buie a
Constables staffe: nay I will be the chiefe of my parish, there
wants nothing but a wench, a cat, a dog, a wife and a seruant, to
make an hole familie, shall I marrie with *Alice*, good mã *Grimshaues*
daughter, shee is faire, but indeede her tongue is like
Clocks on Shrouetuesday, alwaies out of temper? shall I wed
Sisley of the Whightõ? Ohn, o she is like a frog in a parcely bed, |1720|
as scittish as an ele, if I seek to hãper her, she wil horne me: but
a wench must be had maister *Slip.* Yea and shal be deer friend.

And. I now wil driue him from his contemplations. Oh my
mates come forward, the lamb is vnpent, the fox shal preuaile.

> *Enter three Antiques, who dance round, and take*
> *Slipper with them.*

Slip. I will my freend, and I thanke you heartilie, pray keepe
your curtesie, I am yours in the way of an hornepipe, they
are strangers, I see they vnderstand not my language, wee
wee. |1730|

> *VVhilest they are dauncing, Andrew takes away his money,*
> *and the other Antiques depart.*

Slip. Nay but my friends, one hornpipe, further a refluence
backe, and two doubles forward: what not one crosse point against
Sundayes. What ho sirrha, you gone, you with the nose
like an Eagle, and you be a right greeke, one turne more,
theeues theeues, I am robd theeues. Is this the knauerie of Fidlers?
Well, I will then binde the hole credit of their occupatiõ
on a bagpiper, and he for my money, but I will after, and
teach them to caper in a halter, that haue cousoned me of my |1740|
money.

Exeunt.

Enter Nano, Dorothea, *in mans apparell.* IV. iv.

Doro. Ah *Nano*, I am wearie of these weedes,
Wearie to weeld this weapon that I bare:
Wearie of loue, from whom my woe proceedes.
Wearie of toyle, since I haue lost my deare,
O wearie life, where wanted no distresse,
But euery thought is paide with heauinesse.

Na. Too much of wearie madame, if you please, 1750
Sit downe, let wearie dye, and take your ease.

Dorot. How looke I *Nano* like a man or no?

Nano. If not a man, yet like a manlie shrowe.

Doro. If any come and meete vs on the way,
What should we do if they inforce vs stay.

Na. Set cap a huffe, and challenge him the field,
Suppose the worst, the weake may fight to yeeld.

Dorot. The battaile *Nano* in this troubled minde,
Is farre more fierce then euer we may finde.
The bodies wounds by medicines may be eased, 1760
But griefes of mindes, by salues are not appealed.

Na. Say Madame, will you heare your *Nano* sing?

Dor. Of woe good boy, but of no other thing:

Na. What if I sing of fancie will it please?

Dor. To such as hope successe, such noats breede ease.

Na. What if I sing like *Damon* to my sheepe?

Dor. Like *Phillis* I will sit me downe to weepe.

Na. Nay since my songs afford such pleasure small,
Ile sit me downe, and sing you none at all.

Doro. Oh be not angrie *Nano.* 1770

Nano. Nay you loath,
To thinke on that, which doth content vs both.

Doro. And how?

Nano. You scorne desport when you are wearie,

50

And loath my mirth, who liue to make you merry.

Doro. Danger and fear withdraw me from delight.

Na. Tis vertue to contemne fals Fortunes spight.

Do. What shuld I do to please thee friendly squire?

Na. A smile a day, is all I will require:
And if you pay me well the smiles you owe me, 1780
Ile kill this cursed care, or else beshrowe me.

Doug. We are descried, oh *Mano* we are dead.

Enter Iaques his sword drawne.

Nano. Tut yet you walk, you are not dead indeed,
Drawe me your sword, if he your way withstand.

Do. And I will seeke for rescue out of hand,
Run *Nano* runne, preuent thy Princes death.

Na. Feare not, ile run all danger out of breath.

Iaq. Ah you *calletta*, you *strumpet, ta Matressa Doretie este, vous
surprius* come say your pater noster, *car vous est mort par ma foy* 1790

Do. Callet, *me strumpet, Catiue* as thou art
But euen a Princesse borne, who scorne thy threats.
Shall neuer French man say, an English mayd,
Of threats of forraine force will be afraid.

Iaq. You no *dire vostre prieges, vrbleme merchants famme,
guarda* your *bresta, there me make you die on my morglay,*

Doro. God sheeld me haplesse princes and a wife.

They fight, and shee is sore wounded.

And saue my soule, altho I loose my life.
Ah I am slaine, some piteous power repay, 1800
This murtherers cursed deed, that doth me stay.

Iaq. Elle est tout mort, me will runne *pur* a wager, for feare me
be *surpryes* and *pendu* for my labour. Be in *Ie meu alera au roy
auy cits me affaires, Ie serra vn chiualier,* for this daies trauaile.

Exit.

Enter Nano, *S. Cutbert Anderson,
his sword drawne.*

S. Cutb. Where is this poore distressed gentleman?

51

Nano. Here laid on ground, and wounded to the death. 1810
Ah gentle heart, how are these beautious lookes,
Dimd by the tyrant cruelties of death:
Oh wearie soule, breake thou from forth my brest,
And ioyne thee with the soule I honoured most.

S. Cut. Leaue mourning friend, the man is yet aliue,
Some helpe me to conuey him to my house:
There will I see him carefully recured,
And send priuie search to catch the murtherer.

Nano. The God of heauen reward the curteous knight.

Exeunt. And they beare out *Dorothea.* 1820

Enter the King of Scots, Iaques, Ateukin, Andrew, Iaques *IV. v.
running with his swoord one way, the King with his
traine an other way.*

K. of S. Stay *Iaques,* feare not, sheath thy murthering blade:
Loe here thy King and friends are come abroad,
To saue thee from the terrors of pursuite:
What is she dead?

Iaq. Wee Monsieur, elle is blesse per lake teste, oues les espanles,
I warrant she no trouble you.

Ateu. Oh then my liege, how happie art thou growne, 1830
How fauoured of the heauens, and blest by loue:
Mee thinkes I see faire *Ida* in thine armes,
Crauing remission for her late attempt,
Mee thinke I see her blushing steale a kisse:
Vniting both your soules by such a sweete,
And you my King suck Nectar from her lips.
Why then delaies your grace to gaine the rest
You long desired? why loose we forward time?
Write, make me spokesman now, vow marriage,
If she deny your fauour let me die. 1840

Andr. Mightie and magnificent potentate, giue credence to
mine honorable good Lord, for I heard the Midwife sweare at
his natiuitie, that the Faieries gaue him the propertie of the
Thracian stone, for who toucheth it, is exempted from griefe,
and he that heareth my Maisters counsell, is alreadle possessed
of happinesse: nay which is more myraculous, as the Noble
man in his infancie lay in his Cradle, a swarme of Bees laid honey

52

on his lippes, in token of his eloquence. *For melle dulcier*
fluit oratio.

Ateu. Your grace must beare with imperfections: 1850
This is exceeding loue that makes him speake.

K. of S. Ateukin I am rauisht in conceit,
And yet deprest againe with earnest thoughts,
Me thinkes this murther soundeth in mine eare,
A threatning noyse of dire and sharp reuenge.
I am incenst with greefe, yet faine would ioy,
What may I do to end me of these doubts?

Ateu. Why Prince it is no murther in a King,
To end an others life to saue his owne,
For you are not as common people bee. 1860
Who die and perish with a fewe mans teares,
But if you faile, the state doth whole default
The Realme is rent in twaine, in such alosse,
And *Aristotle* holdeth this for true,
Of euills needs we must chuse the least,
Then better were it, that a woman died,
Then all the helpe of *Scotland* should be blent,
Tis pollicie my liege, in euerie state,
To cut off members that disturbe the head.
And by corruption generation growes. 1870
And contraries maintaine the world and state.

K. of S. Enough I am confirmed, *Ateukin* come,
Rid me of loue, and rid me of my greefe,
Driue thou the tyrant from this tainted brest,
Then may I triumph in the height of ioy,
Go to mine *Ida*, tell her that I vowe,
To raise her head and make her honours great.
Go to mine *Ida*, tell her that her haires,
Salbe embollished with orient pearles,
And Crownes of Saphyrs compassing her browes, 1880
Shall weare with those sweete beauties of her eyes.
Go to mine *Ida*, tell her that my soule
Shall keepe her semblance closed in my brest,
And I in touching of her milke-white mould,
Will thinke me deified in such a grace:
I like no stay, go write and I will signe.
Reward me *Iaques*, giue him store of Crowne.
And sirrha *Andrew*, scout thou here in Court:

53

And bring me tydings if thou canst perceiue
The least intent of muttering in my traine, 1890
For either those that wrong thy Lord or thee,
Shall suffer death.   *Exit* the King.

Ateu. How much ô mightie king,
Is thy *Ateukin* bound to honour thee:
Bowe thee *Andrew*, bend thine sturdie knees,
Seest thou not here thine onely God on earth?

Iaq. Mes on est mon argent Signior.

Ateu. Come follow me, his graue I see is made,
That thus on suddain he hath left vs here.
Come *Iaques*, we wil haue our packet soone dispatcht 1900
And you shall be my mate vpon the way.

Iaq. Come vous plera Monsieur.

                                        Exeunt.

Andr. Was neuer such a world I thinke before,
When sinners seeme to daunce within a net,
The flatterer and the murtherer they grow big,
By hooke or crooke promotion now is sought,
In such a world where men are so missed,
What should I do? but as the Prouerbe saith,
Runne with the Hare, and hunt with the Hound. 1910
To haue two meanes, beseemes a wittie man:
Now here in Court I may aspire and clime,
By subtiltie for my maisters death.
And if that faile, well fare an other drift:
I will in secret certaine letters send
Vnto the English King, and let him know
The order of his daughters ouerthtow.
That if my maister crack his credit here,
As I am sure long flattery cannot hold,
I may haue meanes within the English Court 1920
To scape the scourge that waits on bad aduice.   *Exit.*

Chorus. V. Chor.

Enter Bohan and Obiron.

Ober. Beleue me bonny Scot, these slrange euents,
Are passing pleasing, may they end as well.

Boha. Else say that *Bohan* hath a barren skull,
If better motions yet then any past,
Do not more glee to make the fairie greet,
But my small son made prittie hansome shift,
To saue the Queene his Mistresse by his speed. 1930

Obiro. Yea you Ladie for his sport he made,
Shall see when least he hopes, Ile stand his friend,
Or else hee capers in a halters end.

Boha. What hang my son? I trowe not *Obiran*:
Ile rather die, then see him woe begon.

Enter a rownd, or some daunce at Pleasure.

Ober. Bohan be pleasd, for do they what they will,
Heere is my hand, Ile saue thy son from ill.

Exit.

Actus Quintus. Schena Prima. V. i.

Enter the Queene in a night gowne, LadieAnderson, 1941
and Nano.

La. And. My gentle friend beware in taking aire,
Your walkes growe not offensiue to your woundes.

Do. Madame I thank you of your courteous care,
My wounds are well nigh clos'd, tho sore they are.

L. And. Me thinks these closed wounds should breed more griefe,
Since open wounds haue cure, and find reliefe.

Dor. Madame, if vndiscouered wounds you meane,
They are not curde, because they are not seene. 1950

L. And. I meane the woundes which do the heart subdue.

Nano. Oh that is loue, Madame speake I not true?

Ladie Anderson ouerheares.

La. And. Say it were true, what salue for such a sore?

55

Nano. Be wise, and shut such neighbours out of dore.

La. And. How if I cannot driue him from my brest?

Nano. Then chaine him well, and let him do his best.

S. Cutb. In ripping vp their wounds, I see their wit,
But if these woundes be cured I sorrow it.

Doro. Why are you so intentiue to behold, 1960
My pale and wofull lookes, by care controld?

La. And. Because in them a readie way is found,
To cure my care, and heale my hidden wound.

Nano. Good Maister shut your eyes, keepe that conceit,
Surgeons giue *Quoine*, to get a good receit.

Doro. Peace wanton son, this Ladie did amend
My woundes: mine eyes her hidden griefe shall end,
Looke not too much, it is a waightie case.

Nano. Where as a man puts on a maidens face,
For many times if Ladies weare them not, 1970
A nine moneths wound with little worke is got.

S. Cutb. Ile breake off their dispute, least loue proceed,
From couert smiles, to perfect loue indeed.

Nano. The cats abroad, stirre not, the mice bee still.

L. And. Tut, wee can flie such cats when so we will.

S. Cutb. How fares my guest, take cheare, nought shall default,
That eyther doth concerne your health or ioy,
Vse me, my house, and what is mine is yours.

Doro. Thankes gentle knight, and if all hopes be true,
I hope ere long to do as much for you. 1980

S. Cutb. Your vertue doth acquite me of that doubt:
But courteous sir, since troubles calles me hence,
I must to *Edenbourg* vnto the king,
There to take charge, and waight him in his warres:
Meane while good Madame take this squire in charge,
And vse him so as if it were my selfe.

L. And. Sir *Cutbert* doubt not of my dilligence:
Meane while, till your returne God send you health.

Doro. God blesse his grace, and if his cause be iust,

Prosper his wartes: if not hee'l mend I trust: 1990
Good sir what mooues the king to fall to armes?

S. Cutb. The king of England forrageth his land,
And hath besieged *Dambac* with mightie force:
What other newes are common in the Court,
Reade you these letters Madame tell the squire,
The whole affaires of state, for I must hence.

Exit.

Doro. God prosper you, and bring you backe from thence:
Madame what newes?

La. And. They say the Queene is slaine. 2000

Doro. Tut, such reports more false then trueth containe.

L. And. but these reports haue made his Nobles leaue him.

Doro. Ah carelesse men, and would they so deceiue him?

La. And. The land is spoylde, the commons fear the crosse,
All crie against the king, their cause of losse:
The English king subdues and conquers all.

Doro. Ah lasse, this warre growes great, on causes small.

L. And. Our Court is desolate, our Prince alone,
Still dreading death.

Doro. Woes me, for him I moane, 2010
Helpe, now helpe, a suddaine qualme
Assayles my heart.

Nano. Good Madame stand her friend,
Giue vs some licor to refresh her heart.

L. And. Daw thou her vp, ande I will fetch thee foorth
Potions of comfort to represse h r paine.

Exit.

Nano. Fie Princesse, faint on euery fond report,
How well nigh had you opened your effate:
Couer these sorrowes with the vaile of ioy, 2020
And hope the best, for why this warre will cause,
A great repentance in your husbands minde.

Doro. Ah *Nano*, trees liue not without their sap,
And *Clitia* cannot blush but on the sunne,
The thirstie earth is broke with many a gap,

57

And lands are leane, where riuers do not runne,
Where soule is reft from that it loueth best,
How can it thriue or boast of quiet rest?
Thou knowest the Princes losse must be my death,
His griefe, my griefe: his mischiefe must be mine: 2030
Oh if thou loue me, *Nano* high to court,
Tell *Rosse*, tell *Bartram* that I am aliue,
Conceale thou yet, the place of my aboade,
Will them euen as they loue their Queene,
As they are charie of my soule and ioy,
To guard the King, to serue him as my Lord:
Haste thee good *Nana*, for my husbands care,
Consumeth mee and wounds mee to the heart.

    Nano. Madame I go, yet loth to leaue you heere.

Exeunt. 2040

    Dor. Go thou with speed, euen as thou holdst me deare,
Returne in haste.

    Enter Ladie Anderson.

    L. An. Now sir, what cheare? come tast this broth I bring.

    Doro. My griefe is past, I feele no further sting.

    L. And. Where is your dwarfe? Why hath hee left you sir?

    Doro. For some affaires, hee is not traueld farre.

    L. And. If so you please, come in and take your rest.

    Doro. Feare keepes awake a discontented brest.

Exeunt. 2050

    *After a solemne seruice, enter from the widdowes house a seruice, V. ii.
musical songs of marriages, or a maske, or what prettie
triumph you list, to them, Ateukin and Gnato.*

    Ate. What means this triumph frend? why are these feasts?

    Serui. Faire *Ida* sir, was marryed yesterday,
Vnto sir *Eustace*, and for that intent,
Wee feast and sport it thus to honour them:
And if you please, come in and take your part,
My Ladie is no niggard of her cheare.   *Exit.*

    Iaq. Monsigneur, why be you so sadda, *fette bon chere fontre* 2060 *de ce monde.*

   Ateu. What? was I borne to bee the scorne of kinne?
To gather feathers like to a hopper crowe,
And loose them in the height of all my pompe:
Accursed man now is my credite lost:
Where is my vowes I made vnto the king?
What shall become of mee, if hee shall heare,
That I haue causde him kill a vertuous Queene?
And hope in vaine for that which now is lost:
Where shall I hide my head? I knowe the heauens 2070
Are iust, and will reuenge: I know my sinnes
Exceede compare: should I proceed in this?
This *Eustace* must a man be made away:
Oh were I dead, how happy should I bee?

   Iaq. Est ce donque a tell poynt vostre estat, faith then
adeiu *Scotland,* adeiu *Signior Ateukin,* me will homa
to *France,* and no be hanged in a strange country.   *Exit.*

   Ateu. Thou doest me good to leaue me thus alone,
That galling griefe and I may yoake in one:
Oh what are subtile meanes to clime on high? 2080
When euery fall swarmes with exceeding shame?
I promist *Idaes* loue vnto the Prince,
But shee is lost, and I am false forsworne:
I practis'd *Dorotheas* haplesse death,
And by this practise haue commenst a warre.
Oh cursed race of men that traficque guile,
And in the end, themselues and kings beguile:
A shamde to looke vpon my Prince againe:
A shamde of my suggestions and aduise:
A shamde of life: a shamde that I haue erde: 2090
Ile hide my selfe, expecting for my shame.
Thus God doth worke with those, that purschase fame
By flattery, and make their Prince their gaine.   *Exeunt.*

Enter the King of England, Lord Percey, Samles, and others. V. iii.

   Arius. Thus farre the English Peeres haue we displayde,
Our wauing Ensignes with a happy warre,
Thus neerely hath our furious rage reuengde,
My daughters death vpon the traiterous Scot,
And now before *Dambar* our campe is pitcht,
Which if it yeeld not to our compremise, 2100

The place shall furrow where the pallace stood,
And furie shall enuy so high a power,
That mercie shall bee bannisht from our swords.

   Doug. What seekes the English King?

   Arius. Scot open those gates, and let me enter in,
Submit thy selfe and thine vnto my grace,
Or I will put each mothers sonne to death,
And lay this Cittie leuell with the ground.

   Doug. For what offence? for what default of ours?
Art thou incenst so sore against our state? 2110
Can generous hearts in nature bee so sterne
To pray on those that neuer did offend?
What tho the Lyon, (king of brutish race,
Through outrage sinne, shall lambes be therefore slaine?
Or is it lawfull that the humble die,
Because the mightie do gainsay the right?
O English King, thou bearest in thy brest,
The King of beasts, that harmes not yeelding ones,
The Roseall crosse is spred within thy field,
A signe of peace, not of reuenging warre: 2120
Be gracious then vnto this little towne,
And tho we haue withstood thee for a while,
To shew alleageance to our liefest liege,
Yet since wee know no hope of any helpe,
Take vs to mercie, for wee yeeld our selues.

   Ari. What shall I enter then and be your Lord?

   Doug. We will submit vs to the English king.

   They descend downe, open the gates, and humble them.

   Arius. Now life and death dependeth on my sword:
This hand now reard, my *Douglas* if I list, 2130
Could part thy head and shoulders both in twaine:
But since I see thee wise and olde in yeares,
True to thy king, and faithfull in his warres,
Liue thou and thine, *Dambar* is too too small,
To giue an entrance to the English king,
I Eaglelike disdaine these little soules,
And looke on none but those that dare resist,
Enter your towne as those that liue by me,
For others that resist, kill, forrage, spoyle:
Mine English souldiers, as you loue your king,

Reuenge his daughters death, and do me right.

Exeunt,

Enter the Lawyer, the Merchant, and the Diuine. V. iv.

Lawyer. My friends, what thinke you of this present state,
Were euer seene such changes in a time?
The manners and the fashions of this age,
Are like the *Ermine* skinne so full of spots,
As soone may the Moore bee washed white,
Then these corruptions bannisht from this Realme.

Merch. What sees mas Lawyer in this state amisse? 2150

Law. A wresting power that makes a nose of wax,
Of grounded lawe, a damde and subtile drift,
In all estates to clime by others losse,
An eager thrift of wealth, forgetting trueth,
Might I ascend vnto the highest states,
And by discent discouer euery crime,
My friends I should lament, and you would greeue
To see the haplesse ruines of this Realme.

Diu. O Lawyer, thou haste curious eyes to prie,
Into the secrets maimes of their estate, 2160
But if thy vaile of error were vnmaskt,
Thy selfe should see your sect, do maime her most:
Are you not those that should maintaine the peace,
Yet onely are the patrones of our strife?
If your profession haue his ground and spring,
First from the lawes of God, then countriees right,
Not any waies inuerting natures power,
Why thriue you by contentions? Why deuise you
Clawses, and subtile reasons toexcept:
Our state was first before you grew so great, 2170
A Lanterne to the world for vnitie:
Now they that are befriended, and are rich,
Or presse the poore, come *Homer* without quoine,
He is not heard: What shall we terme this drift?
To say the poore mans cause is good and iust,
And yet the rich man gaines the best in lawe:
It is your guise, (the more the world laments)
To quoine *Prouisoes* to beguile your lawes,
To make a gay pretext of due proceeding,

When you delay your common pleas for yeares: 2180
Mark what these dealings lately here haue wroght:
The craftie men haue purchaste greatmens lands
They powle, they pinch, their tennants are vndone:
If these complaine by you they are vndone,
You fleese them of their quoine, their children beg,
And many want, because you may bee rich,
This scarre is mightie maister Lawyer,
Now man hath gotten head within this land,
Marke but the guise, the poore man that is wrongd,
Is readie to rebell: hee spoyles, he pilles, 2190
We need no foes to forrage that wee haue,
The lawe (say they) in peace consumed vs,
And now in warre wee will consume the lawe:
Looke to this mischiefe, Lawyers conscience knowes
You liue amisse, amend it, least you end.

    Law. Good Lord, that their Diuines should see so farre
In others faults, without amending theirs?
Sir, sir, the generall defaults in state,
(If you would read before you did correct)
Are by a hidden working from aboue, 2200
By their successiue changes still remainde,
Were not the lawe by contraries maintainde,
How could the trueth from falsehood be discernde?
Did wee not tast the bitternesse of warre?
How could wee knowe the sweet effects of peace?
Did wee not feele the nipping winter frostes,
How should we know the sweetnesse of the spring?
Should all things still remaine in one estate,
Should not in greatest arts some scarres be found,
Were all vpright and changd, what world were this? 2210
A *Chaos*, made of quiet, yet no world,
Because the parts thereof did still accord,
This matter craues a variance not a speech,
But sir Diuine to you, looke on your maimes,
Diuisions, sects, your summonies and bribes:
Your cloaking with the great, for feare to fall,
You shall perceiue you are the cause of all.
Did each man know there were a storme at hand,
Who would not cloath him well, to shun the wet?
Did Prince and Peere, the Lawyer and the least, 2220
Know what were sinne, without a partiall glose,

Wee need no long discouery then of crimes,
For each would mend, aduis'de by holy men:
Thus but slightly shadow out your sinnes,
But if they were depainted out for life,
Alasse wee both had wounds inough to heale.

    Merch. None of you both I see but are in fault,
Thus simple men as I do swallow flies,
This graue Diuine can tell vs what to do,
But wee may say: Phisitian mend thy selfe, 2230
This Lawyer hath a pregnant wit to talke,
But all are words, I see no deeds of woorth.

    Law. Good Merchant lay your fingers on your mouth,
Be not a blab, for feare you bite your selfe,
What should I terme your state, but euen the way
To euery ruine in this Common-weale,
You bring vs in the meanes of all excesse,
You rate it, and retalde it as you please,
You sweare, forsweare, and all to compasse wealth,
Your mony is your God, your hoord your heauen, 2240
You are the groundworke of contention:
First heedlesse youth, by you is ouerreacht,
Wee are corrupted by your many crownes:
The Gentlemen, whose titles you haue bought,
Loose all their fathers toyle within a day,
Whilst *Hob* your sonne, and *Sib* your nutbrowne childe,
Are Gentle folkes, and Gentles are beguilde:
This makes so many Noble maides to stray,
And take sinister courses in the state.   *Enter a Scout.*

    Scout. My friends begone and if you loue your liues, 2250
The King of England marcheth heere at hand,
Enter the campe for feare you bee surprisde.

    Diuine. Thankes gentle scout, God mend that is amisse,
And place true, zeale whereas corruption is.   *.Exeun..*

Enter Dorothea, Ladie Anderson and Nano. v. v.

    Doro. What newes in Court, *Nano* let vs know it?

    Nano. If so you please my Lord, I straight will shew it:
The English king hath all the borders spoyld,
Hath taken *Morton* prisoner, and hath slaine
Seuen thousand Scottish Lords, not sarre from *Twearde.* 2260

Doro. A wofull murther, and a bloodie deed.

Nano. Thinking our liege hath sought by many meanes
For to appease his enemie by prayers,
Nought will preuaile vnlesse hee can restore,
Faire *Dorothea* long supposed dead:
To this intent he hath proclaimed late,
That who so euer returne the Queene to Court,
Shall haue a thousand Markes for his reward.

L. And. He loues her then I see, altho inforst,
That would bestow such gifts for to regaine her: 2270
Why sit you sad, good sir be not dismaide.

Na. Ile lay my life this man would be a maide.

Dor. Faine would I shewe my selfe, and change my tire.

And. Whereon diuine you sir?

Na. Vppon desire.
Madam marke but my skill, ile lay my life,
My maister here, will prooue a married wife.

Doro. Wilt thou bewray me *Nano*?

Nano. Madam no:
You are a man, and like a man you goe. 2280
But I that am in speculation seene,
Know you would change your state to be a Queene.

Dor. Thou art not dwarffe to learne thy mistresse mind:
Faine would I with thy selfe disclose my kind,
But yet I blush.

Na. What blush you Madam than,
To be your selfe, who are a fayned man?
Let me alone.

La. And. Deceitfull beautie hast thou scornd me so?

Nano. Nay muse not maiden, for she tels you true. 2290

La. An. Beautie bred loue, and loue hath bred my shame.

N. And womens faces work more wrongs then these:
Take comfort Madam to cure our disease.
And yet he loues a man as well as you,
Onely this difference, she cannot fancie too.

La. An. Blush, greeue, and die, in thine insaciat lust.

Do. Nay liue and ioy that thou hast won a friend,
That loues thee as his life, by god desert.

La. And. I ioy my Lord more then my tongue can tell:
Alhough not as I desir'd, I loue you well: 2300
But modestie, that neuer blusht before,
Discouer my false heart. I say no more.
Let me alone.

Doro. Good *Nano* stay a while.
Were I not sad, how kindlie could I smile,
To see how faine I am to leaue this weede:
And yet I faint to shewe my selfe indeede.
But danger hates delay, I will be bold,
Faire Ladie I am not, suppose
A man, but euen that Qeene, more haplesse I, 2310
Whom Scottish King appointed hath to die:
I am the haplesse Princesse, for whose right,
These kings in bloudie warres reuenge dispight.
I am that *Dorothea* whom they seeke,
Yours bounden for your kindnesse and releefe:
And since you are the meanes that saue my life,
Your selfe and I will to the Camp repaire,
Whereas your husband shal enioy reward,
And bring me to his highnesse once againe.

An. Pardon most gratious Princesse, if you please, 2320
My rude discourse and homelie entertaine,
And if my words may sauour any worth,
Vouchsafe my counsaile in this waightie cause:
Since that our liege hath so vnkindly dealt:
Giue him no trust, returne vnto your syre,
There may you safelie liue in spight of him.

Doro. Ah Ladie, so wold worldly counsell work,
But constancie, obedience, and my loue,
In that my husband is my Lord and chiefe,
These call me to compassion of his estate, 2330
Disswade me not, for vertue will not change,

An. What woonderous constancie is this I heare?
If English dames their husbands loue so deer,
I feare me in the world they haue no peere.

Na. Come Princes wend, and let vs change your weede,

I long to see you now a Queene indeede.

Exeunt.

Enter the King of Scots, the English Herauld & Lords. V. vi.

K. of S. He would haue parly Lords, Herauld say he shall,
And get thee gone: goe leaue me to my selfe: 2340
Twixt loue and feare, continuall is the warres:
The one assures me of my *Idaes* loue,
The other moues me for my murthred Queene.
Thus finde I greefe of that whereon I ioy,
And doubt, in greatest hope, and death in weale,
Ah lasse what hell may be compared with mine,
Since in extreames my comforts do consist?
Warre then will cease, when dead ones are reuiued.
Some then will yeelde, when I am dead for hope.
Who doth disturbe me? *Andrew?* 2350

Andrew enter with Slipper.

Andr. I my liege.

K. of S. What newes?

Andr. I thinke my mouth was made at first,
To tell these tragique tales my liefest Lord.

K. of S. What is *Ateukin* dead, tell me the worst?

Andr. No but your *Ida*, shall I tell him all?
Is married late (ah shall I say to whom?)
My maister sad: (for why he shames the Court)
Is fled away? ah most vnhappie flight. 2360
Onelie my selfe, ah who can loue you more?
To shew my dutie (dutie past beliefe)
Am come vnto your grace (oh gratious liege)
To let you know, oh would it weare not thus,
That loue is vain, and maids soone lost and wonne.

K. of S. How haue the partial heauens thē dealt with me,
Boading my weale, for to abase my power?
Alas what thronging thoughts do me oppresse?
Iniurious loue is partiall in my right,
And flattering tongues by whom I was misled, 2370
Haue laid a snare to spoyle my state and me.
Methinkes I heare my *Dorotheas* goast,

Howling reuenge for my accursed hate,
The gifts of those my subiects that are slaine,
Pursue me crying out, woe, woe, to lust,
The foe pursues me at my pallace doore:
He breakes my rest and spoyles me in my Camp,
Ah flattering broode of *Sicophants* my foes,
First shall my dire reuenge begin on you,
I will reward thee *Andrew*. 2380

Slip. Nay sir if you be in your deeds of charitie, remember me
I rubd M. *Ateukins* horse heeles, when he rid to the medowes.

K. of S. And thou shalt haue thy recompence for that.
Lords beare them to the prison, chaine them fast,
Vntil we take some order for their deathes.

And. If so your grace in such sort giue rewards,
Let me haue nought, I am content to want.

Slip. Then I pray sir giue me all, I am as ready for a reward as
an oyster for a fresh tide, spare not me sir.

K. of S. Then hang them both as traitors to the King. 2390

Slip. The case is altered, sir, ile none of your gifts, what I take
a reward at your hands? Maister, faith sir no: I am a man of a
better conscience.

K. of S. Why dallie you? go draw them hence away.

Slip. Why alas sir, I wil go away I thanke you gentle friends,
I pray you spare your pains, I will not trouble his honors maistership,
ile run away.

> Enter Adam, *and Antiques, and carrie away the Clowne,*
> *he makes pots, and sports, and scornes.*

Why stay you? moue me not, let search be made, 2400
For vile *Ateukin*, who so findes him out,
Shall haue fiue hundreth markes for his reward.
Away with the Lords troupes about my tent,
Let all our souldiers stand in battaile ray,
For lo the English to their parley come.

> March ouer brauelie *first the English hoste, the sword caried*
> *before the King by Percy. The Scottish on the other side,*
> *with all their pompe brauelie.*

K. of S. What seekes the King of *England* in this land?

67

K. of Eng. False traiterous Scot, I come for to reuenge 2410
My daughters death: I come to spoyle thy wealth,
Since thou hast spoyld me of my marriage ioy.
I come to heape thy land with Carkasses,
That this thy thriftie soyle choakt vp with blood,
May thunder forth reuenge vpon thy head.
I come to quit thy louelesse loue with death,
In briefe, no meanes of peace shall ere be found,
Except I haue my daughter or thy head.

K. of S. My head proud King? abase thy prancking plaines,
So striuing fondly, maiest thou catch thy graue. 2420
But if true iudgement do direct thy course,
These lawfull reasons should deuide the warre,
Faith not by my consent thy daughter dyed.

K. of E. Thou liest false Scot, thy agẽts haue cõfest it.
These are but fond delayes, thou canst not thinke
A meanes for to reconcile me for thy friend,
I haue thy parasites confession pend:
What then canst thou alleage in thy excuse?

K. of S. I will repay the raunsome for her bloud.

K. of E. What thinkst thou catiue, I wil sel my child, 2430
No if thou be a Prince and man at armes,
In singule combat come and trie thy right,
Else will I prooue thee recreant to thy face.

K. of S. I tooke no combat false iniurious King,
But since thou needlesse art inclinde to warre,
Do what thou darest we are in open field.
Arming thy battailes I will fight with thee.

K. of E. Agreed, now ttumpets sound a dreadfull charge
Fight for your Princesse, braue English men:
Now for your lands your children and your wiues, 2440
My Scottish Peeres, and lastly for your King.

*Alarũ soũded, both the battailes offer to meet, & as the
Kings are ioyning battaile, Enter sir Cutber tohis Lady
Cutbert, with the Queene Dorothea richly attired.*

S. Cut. Stay Princes wage not warre, a priuie grudge
Twixt such as you (most high in Maiestie)
Afflicts both nocent and the innocent,
How many swordes deere Princes see I drawne?

The friend against his friend, a deadly friend:
A desperate diuision in those lands, 2450
Which if they ioyne in one, commaund the world.
Oh stay with reason mittigate your rage,
And let an old man humbled on his knees,
Intreat a boone good Princes of you both.

   K. of En. I condiscend, for why thy reuerend years
Import some newes of truth and consequence,
I am content, for *Anderson* I know.

   K. of S. Thou art my subiect and doest meane me good.

   S. Cut. And. But by your gratious fauours grant me this,
To sweare vpon your sword to do me right. 2460

   K. of Eng. See by my sword, and by a Princes faith,
In euery lawfull sort I am thine owne.

   K. of S. And by my Scepter and the Scortish Crowne,
I am resolu'd to grant thee thy request.

   Cutb. I see you trust me Princes who repose,
The waight of such a warre vpon my will.
Now marke my sute, a tender Lyons whelpe,
This other day came stragling in the woods,
Attended by a young and tender hinde,
In courage hautie, yet tyred like a lambe, 2470
The Prince of beasts had left this young in keepe,
To foster vp as louemate and compeere,
Vnto the Lyons mate a naibour friend,
This stately guide seduced by the fox,
Sent forth an eger Woolfe bred vp in *France*,
That gript the tender whelp, and wounded it.
By chance as I was hunting in the woods,
I heard the moane the hinde made for the whelpe,
I tooke them both, and brought them to my house,
With charie care I haue recurde the one, 2480
And since I know the lyons are at strife,
About the losse and dammage of the young,
I bring her home, make claime to her who list.

   Hee discouereth her.

   Doro. I am the whelpe, bred by this Lyon vp,
This royall English king my happy sire,

Poore *Nano* is the hinde that tended me:
My father Scottish king, gaue me to thee:
A haplesse wife, thou quite misled by youth,
Haste fought sinister loues and forraine ioyes, 2490
The fox *Ateukin*, cursed Parasite,
Incenst your grace to send the woolfe abroad,
The French borne *Iaques*, for to end my daies,
Hee traiterous man, pursued me in the woods,
And left mee wounded, where this noble knight,
Both rescued me and mine, and sau'd my life.
Now keep thy promise, *Dorothea* liues:
Giue *Anderson* his due and iust reward:
And since you kings, your warres began by me,
Since I am safe, returne surcease your fight. 2500

   K. of S. Durst I presume to looke vpon those eies,
Which I haue tired with a world of woes,
Or did I thinke submission wereynough,
Or sighes might make an entrance to my soule:
You heauens, you know how willing I wold weep:
You heauens can tell, how glad I would submit:
You heauens can say, how firmly I would sigh.

   Do. Shame me not Prince, companion in thy bed,
Youth hath missed: tut but a little fault,
Tis kingly to amend what is amisse: 2510
Might I with twise as many paines as these,
Vnite our hearts, then should my wedded Lord,
See how incessaunt labours I would take.
My gracious father gouerne your affects,
Giue me that hand, that oft hath blest this head,
And claspe thine armes, that haue embraced this,
About the shoulders of my wedded spouse:
Ah mightie Prince, this king and I am one,
Spoyle thou his subiects, thou despoylest me:
Touch thou his brest, thou doest attaint this heart, 2520
Oh bee my father then in louing him.

   K. of Eng. Thou prouident kinde mother of increase,
Thou must preuaile, ah nature thou must rule:
Holde daughter, ioyne my hand and his in one,
I will embrace him for to fauour thee,
I call him friend, and take him for my sonne.

   Dor. Ah royall husband, see what God hath wrought,

70

Thy foe is now thy friend: good men at armes,
Do you the like, these nations if they ioyne,
What Monarch with his leigemen in this world, 2530
Dare but encounter you in open fielde?

K. of S. Al wisedome ioynde with godly pietie,
Thou English king, pardon my former youth,
And pardon courteous Queen my great misdeed:
And for assurance of mine after life,
I take religious vowes before my God,
To honour thee for fauour, her for wife.

L. And. But yet my boones good Princes are not past,
First English king I humbly do request,
That by your meanes our Princesse may vnite, 2540
Her loue vnto mine alder truest loue,
Now you will loue, maintaine and helpe them both.

K. of Eng. Good *Anderson*, I graunt thee thy request.

L. And. But you my Prince must yeelde me mickle more:
You know your Nobles are your chiefest ffaies,
And long time haue been bannisht from your Court,
Embrace and reeoncile them to your selfe:
They are your hands, whereby you oght to worke.
As for *Ateukin*, and his lewde compeeres,
That sooth'd you in your sinnes and youthly pompe, 2550
Exile, torment, and punish such as they,
For greater vipers neuer may be found
Within a date, then such aspiring heads,
That reck not how they clime, so that they clime.

K. of S. Guid Knight I graunt thy sute, first I submit
And humble craue a pardon of your grace:
Next courteous Queene, I pray thee by thy loues,
Forgiue mine errors past, and pardon mee.
My Lords and Princes, if I haue misdone,
(As I haue wrongd indeed both you and yours) 2560
Heereafter trust me, you are deare to me:
As for *Auteukin*, who so findes the man,
Let him haue Martiall lawe, and straight be hangd,
As (all his vaine arbetters now are diuided)
And *Anderson* our Treasurer shall pay,
Three thousand Markes, for friendly recompence.

L. Andr. But Princes whilst you friend it thus in one,

Me thinks of friendship, *Nano* shall haue none.

 Doro. What would my Dwarfe, that I will not bestow?

 Nano. My boone faire Queene is this, that you would go, 2570
Altho my bodie is but small and neate,
My stomacke after toyle requireth meate,
An easie sute, dread Princes will you wend?

 K. of S. Art thou a Pigmey borne my prettie frend?

 Nano. Not so great King, but nature when she framde me,
Was scant of earth, and *Nano* therefore namde me:
And when she sawe my bodie was so small,
She gaue me wit to make it big withall.

 K. Till time when, *Dor.* Eate then.

 K. My friend it stands with wit, 2580
To take repast when stomacke serueth it.

 Dor. Thy pollicie my *Nano* shall preuaile:
Come royall father, enter we my tent:
And souldiers feast it, frolike it like friends,
My Princes bid this kinde and courteous traine,
Partake some fauours of our late accord.
Thus warres haue end, and after dreadfull hate,
Men learne at last to know their good estate. *Exeunt.*

FINIS.

Lightning Source UK Ltd.
Milton Keynes UK
UKHW012213100820
367994UK00009B/1095